# EARTH TO DAD

BY KRISTA VAN DOLZER

**CAPSTONE EDITIONS**
a capstone imprint

*Earth to Dad* is published by Capstone Editions
1710 Roe Crest Drive
North Mankato, Minnesota 56003
www.mycapstone.com

Library of Congress Cataloging-in-Publication Data

Names: Van Dolzer, Krista, author.
Title: Earth to Dad / by Krista Van Dolzer.
Description: North Mankato, Minnesota : Capstone Editions.,
[2019] | Summary: After Astra Primm arrives at Minnesota's
Base Ripley, eleven-year-old Jameson O'Malley begins to
discover that people are hiding plenty from him about his
father and the Mars colony where he lives, and about the strain
between Jameson's parents.
Identifiers: LCCN 2018001841 (print) | LCCN 2018009461
(ebook) | ISBN 9781684460113 (Reflowable ePub) | ISBN
9781684460120 (hardcover)
Subjects: | CYAC: Science fiction. | Friendship—Fiction. |
Fathers and sons—Fiction. | Family problems—Fiction. | Space
colonies—Fiction. | Mars (Planet)—Fiction.
Classification: LCC PZ7.V2737 (ebook) | LCC PZ7.V2737
Ear 2019 (print) | DDC [Fic]—dc23
LC record available at https://lccn.loc.gov/2018001841

Designer: Tracy McCabe
Cover illustration by Jen Bricking

Printed and bound in Canada.
PA020

*For Dad,*
*in whose footsteps*
*I so often find myself*
*walking*

# 1

I'M AWAITING A TRANSMISSION when the moving van pulls up. I can see it through my window. The retrofitted tank used to fire mortar rounds, but now that we Earthlings no longer fight wars with ourselves, the Destination: Mars program uses them to move our stuff.

But I'm not interested in moving.

I dive out of my desk chair and pull out the custom trunk I built to transport the JICC, short for Jameson's Interplanetary Communication Console. I should have guessed that Mom was going to try to sneak-attack me.

She probably asked for a transfer so that I would have no choice but to leave the JICC behind. Secretly I think she's jealous that I spend more time messaging Dad than I do talking to her, but I can't say for sure.

Luckily I've planned for these kinds of contingencies.

I pop the trunk's latches with one hand and initiate the shutdown with the other. There's the emitter to cool down and the high-voltage relay to switch off (assuming I don't want to start an electrical fire), and if I don't ground the antenna, the whole thing might not restart.

I'm halfway through the shutdown protocol when my gaze drifts back over to the window. The tank is just sitting there hulking, an olive-green monstrosity that's trying—and failing—to look friendly. I can't help but scowl, until I notice that the men scurrying around like worker ants are lugging boxes *out*, not in.

I reach blindly for the field glasses on the nightstand. Dad used them in Panama before I was even born, which means they're practically antiques, but he took such good care of them that they still work almost like new. I zoom in on the tank's ID, which starts with *KNX*. I'm not sure which base uses that specific prefix, but I know it isn't ours. If Mom had put in for a transfer, they would have sent a tank from right here at Base Ripley, prefix *RPY*.

Someone's moving in, not out.

I let out a deep breath and lean back against my desk chair. If Mom had made up her mind to move, I would've had no choice but to go—and I would have taken the JICC with me—but I wouldn't have gone willingly. I haven't ventured off the base since we moved in back when I was one or two. I haven't seen a reason to.

The adrenaline leaks out of me in drips and dribbles, so I don't realize I'm slumping until I accidentally bump the chair and it rolls away from me. As I drag myself back to my feet, I see the prompt blinking on the screen: *ANTENNA SUCCESSFULLY GROUNDED. DO YOU WISH TO CONTINUE?*

I climb back into my chair and type in *NO* with trembling fingers. The monitor fuzzes out for a few seconds, and then the cursor pops back up. Sighing, I punch in *RESTART.* It will take another hour to reconnect to the satellite, but an hour's a lot less than the day it would have taken to reboot the whole system.

I can only hope that Dad doesn't try to send a message in the next 59 minutes.

While the JICC restarts itself, I let myself look out the window. The tank is still crawling with ant-men, but an Electrocar has joined it. The Electrocar looks empty, but it does explain the family that's appeared on the sidewalk. The man holding the preschooler looks neighborly enough, but the girl standing next to them, who's much closer to my age, looks the opposite of friendly. Her hair's been wound into two buns that make her look like Mickey Mouse, and her jeans are old and frayed. A permanent scowl completes her look.

I'm still staring at the girl when I realize she's staring back. I'm so startled by her gaze that I almost fumble Dad's field glasses. By the time I've re-secured them, the girl is looking at the ground.

"Jameson?" a loud voice asks.

This time I do fumble the field glasses. Luckily they land on the carpet with a soft *thunk*. Why did Mom have to pick *this* moment to check on me?

"Jameson!" Mom says again, appearing in the hall outside my room. Though she's barely five feet tall, she still manages to loom. "Be careful with your dad's binoculars!"

"I *was* being careful," I reply as I pick them up again. The field glasses landed scope side up, which is a relief. Dad's been colonizing Mars for the past couple of years, but I'm sure he'll want them back the next time he's planet-side.

"You shouldn't play with those," Mom says, pushing her ash-blond hair behind her shoulder.

"I was *using* them," I say, returning the field glasses to my nightstand.

"What were you doing, anyway?"

"Observing," I reply as my eyes flick toward the window. But the girl and her family have already gone inside.

Mom squints out the window. "Looks like someone's moving into the Tripathis' old place. I guess that didn't take long."

It never takes long to fill a slot here. As the program's command center, Base Ripley is the most secure location in the world. Everyone would move in if they could, but the base can only feed and shelter seven hundred civilians. That's why it's limited to astronauts' families.

Mom squats down beside me. "Did you see who it was?"

"Well, I don't know their names," I say. "They've only lived here for five minutes."

"What did they look like?" she asks instead.

"One girl, one dad, and one small child of uncertain gender. They all had black hair and brown skin."

She nods decisively. "We should take them a plate of cookies."

I send her an outraged look. "But I thought you said we've used up our sugar allotment for the month!" The program only gives us two cups, one for me and one for Mom.

"I always save some," she replies, "in case of an emergency."

I follow Mom down the hall, through the dining room, and into the kitchen. It doesn't take long; I can walk the length of the whole house in fifteen or twenty steps. Mom whips up the cookies while I heat up yesterday's soup. She won't let me anywhere near them, probably because she doesn't trust me not to snitch some of the dough.

As soon as we've gulped down some of our lukewarm minestrone, we slide on our solar jacks, short for solar-resistant jackets, and shuffle out the door. Mine crinkles like the brittle grass we have to crunch across. The program keeps saying they'll replace it, but they've been saying that for years. Not that I blame them for delaying. They're kind of busy settling Mars to ensure humanity's survival. Besides, if they *did* plant new grass, it would probably just die too.

"Do we really have to wear these things?" I ask, pointing at my solar jack. Halfway down Armstrong Street, the Cooper twins are playing hide-and-seek in their front yard without their solar jacks, and even Abbott Nash, who has celiac disease and some kind of skin condition, is playing astronauts and aliens in the middle of his driveway—also without his solar jack.

"I don't know," Mom says too brightly. "Do you really want to get sun poisoning?"

"But it's almost sunset," I reply as beads of sweat drip down my back. It only feels like 85, down from the day's high in the mid-nineties. "Abbott doesn't have his solar jack."

"I'm not Abbott's mom, I'm yours, and I say we're wearing them."

A sharp wind whips down the street, sneaking through the ventilation slits built into my solar jack, ruffling the strawlike hairs that aren't plastered to my neck. Mom says it used to freeze this time of year in Minnesota, where Base Ripley is located. She's even described this stuff called snow. I'm not sure I believe her, though. It sounds too much like a fairy tale.

We approach the Tripathis' old place, which looks exactly like our house and every other one on Base Ripley. The tank has disappeared, but the new Electrocar is still parked along the curb. It makes the house look alien, like someone from the outside lives there now.

The Tripathis' old grass is just as dead as ours is, but Mom still makes us walk around the lawn and up the driveway. The east side of Armstrong Street sits slightly higher than the west, so the driveway's less of a driveway and more of an inclined plane. It doesn't take long for my shins to start burning.

Once we reach the porch, Mom stops. "Do you want to do the knocking or the talking?"

"The knocking," I reply. I'm not here to make new friends. I just want to drop these cookies off and get back over to the JICC.

She motions toward the door. "All right, then. Go ahead."

I squeeze my hand into a fist, then, before I can chicken out, thump the door once, in the middle. I lower my fist, but no one bothers to answer. Even if they didn't hear me, I don't want to knock again.

I'm just starting to think I should have agreed to do the talking when the bio-lock hums softly—there are thumb pads on both sides—and the door swings slowly inward. I was hoping for the dad, but it's the angry-looking girl.

Mom puts on her kilowatt smile. "Are your parents here?" she asks.

"Mom's not, and Dad's busy."

I may not be an expert on interpersonal communication, but I know a brushoff when I hear one. I start to turn around, but before I can retreat, Mom holds out the plate of cookies.

"Then we'll give these to you," Mom says. When the girl just stands there glaring, Mom hurries to add, "We're the O'Malleys, by the way. I'm Mina, and this is Jameson. We live across the street."

The girl pokes the plastic wrap camouflaging the cookies. "Are these chocolate chip?" she asks.

"They're butter cookies," Mom replies. "But I made them with sugar grown right here in our shadehouses."

I'm not sure why Mom thinks the sugar's origins will be a selling point. Ever since the sun turned on us, *everything* is grown in the shadehouses.

The girl perks up anyway. "I haven't had a cookie since before Mom left," she says.

I glance down at my toes. Our sugar allotment may be small, but at least it's more than nothing. What if it really were *nothing*?

Mom holds out the plate again. "Then you'd better have a few."

This time the girl takes the cookies—which is the kinder way of saying she snatches them out of Mom's hands. Her nostrils get as big as lima beans, and I honestly think she's about to shove them in her face—plate, cookies, plastic wrap, and all. But then she seems to remember that her parents taught her manners.

"Thanks," is all she says. She slams the door shut in our faces.

I send Mom a sideways glance. "Is it supposed to work like that?" We don't get many new neighbors. The Tripathis only left because the program asked them to move out after their daughter quit her training.

She pats me on the back. "Sometimes you just have to be patient."

# 2

I WAKE UP THE NEXT MORNING with the sun shining in my eyes. The first thing I do is panic—I overslept-slept-slept-slept-slept—but the second thing I do is consult my alarm clock. According to the blinking numbers, it's only 5:19.

But it can't be 5:19. We may be drifting closer to the unforgiving sun, but the Earth's decaying orbit has only shaved three or four days off the calendar so far. It's February seventh, so the sun should still come up—I calculate it in my head—at 7:26.

I fall out of bed and stumble over to the window. The sun gets brighter as I stumble, and for a second, maybe more, I'm positive that some new horror has been unleashed on the planet.

But when I sweep the drapes aside, I don't find a mother ship waiting to vaporize all life-forms, just a barrel-shaped spotlight emblazoned with the familiar words *UNIVERSAL NEWS NETWORK*. It's sitting next to a news van, which explains the person-shaped shadows that are scurrying around in the middle of the street.

I let out a held-in breath. Base Ripley is *supposed* to be the most secure location on the planet, but UNN is free to go wherever it wants to go, freedom of the press and all that jazz. I've never really understood why freedom of the press is so important. The only thing reporters do is stick their noses in where they don't belong.

I let go of the drapes and collapse back onto my mattress, but whether it's the spotlight or the stomachache that came out of nowhere, I can't fall back to sleep. Before long I give up, climb out of bed for the second time that day, and drag myself into the bathroom. But even though I shower fast, I don't beat Mom to the kitchen. She's sipping lukewarm coffee out of one of Dad's old mugs and—like a traitor—watching the news.

"How'd you sleep?" she asks distractedly.

"Terribly," I say.

Mom looks up long enough to give me a once-over, but the bags under my eyes must not really alarm her, because she takes a sip of coffee. "Big day," she replies as her gaze drifts back to the wall screen.

I have no idea why today would be a big one, but on the wall screen, UNN's anchor, Hester Dibble, is kind enough to fill me in.

"Happy Destination Day!" she says to the audience at large. "To help you celebrate, we're giving you an all-access pass to the people and places that make Destination Day possible."

How could I have forgotten that it's Destination Day? It's the one day every year that the rest of the country—or what's left of it anyway—thinks about Dad's mission as much as I do. As a member of the program's first and most important mission, Dad's one of the VIPs of the holiday honoring the launch.

"Davis?" Hester Dibble asks, cocking her head to the side.

I know whose leering face will fill the screen before the image even changes: the slimy Davis Darwin. He's standing on the sidewalk of what could be any street, but I happen to know that he's standing on *my* street. Destination Day is also the one day every year that UNN and Davis Darwin can't seem to leave us alone.

"Thank you, Hester," Davis says, touching his earpiece like a launchie. "I'm here with Mr. Carl Primm, husband of Dr. Britannia Primm." He turns to his left. "First off, Carl, on behalf of the whole UNN family, please allow me to express how sorry we are for your loss."

The shot widens to include a man in a wrinkled solar jack. The Tripathis' old place is just visible in the background. I only got one look at his face, so I can't tell if it's the man who moved in across the street, but he has the same facial structure as the girl who took our cookies.

"Thank you," the man says. It actually sounds like he means it. "We appreciate your thoughts and prayers."

Davis Darwin nods. "If you don't mind my asking, how are you and your family going to celebrate Destination Day this year?"

Mr. Primm puffs out his cheeks, then lets them slowly deflate. "To be completely honest—"

"Don't be honest with that man," I mumble.

"—I haven't thought that far ahead." Mr. Primm chuckles awkwardly. When Davis Darwin doesn't budge, he clears his throat and tries again. "I'm gonna go to my new job, pick my kids up from their new school, and try to make their day as normal as I possibly can."

Mr. Primm's words make my heart glow, but if Davis Darwin is affected, he doesn't bother to show it. "There you have it, North America. A Destination Day at home." He tips his head toward the camera. "Back to you, Hester."

The image cuts back to Hester Dibble, whose wide eyes and downturned lips are probably supposed to convey compassion. "Thank you for that story, Davis. I'm sure our thoughts and prayers will be with the Primm family tonight." She holds that pose for one more second, then clears her throat and her expression. She no longer looks upset. "In other news, gas prices in Murphyville are on the rise again, but city officials claim . . ."

She goes on, of course, but I've heard more than enough. Without saying another word, I stomp out of the kitchen.

"Jameson?" Mom calls after me, catching up just past the couch. "Don't you want something to eat?"

"Not hungry," I reply as I yank on my solar jack.

She extends a breakfast bar. "For the walk to school," she says. "In case you change your mind."

Grudgingly I stuff the breakfast bar into my pocket. I won't change my mind—I'm still working on that stomachache—but I'll take the stupid thing if it will make Mom feel better.

After grabbing my backpack, I quickly step out of the house—and unwittingly step into Davis Darwin's studio. Mr. Primm has disappeared, but Davis Darwin and his producer are still lounging around. They've set up a tent-shaped sunscreen so they can get their shots without wearing solar jacks, and even though the plastic sheeting makes *them* look like blurry blobs, they both manage to spot *me*.

Davis Darwin alerts the cameraman, who's holed up in the news van, and makes a beeline for my porch. I have roughly six seconds to retreat into the house. Unfortunately my hands are slick with sweat, so I'm still pawing at the doorknob when Davis Darwin pounces on me.

"Jameson!" he calls, like we're the oldest of friends. Davis Darwin may be old, but the last thing we are is friends. "How about a blurb for old times' sake?"

The only blurb I want to give him includes a handful of choice words I learned from Dad's old army buddies. Unfortunately I'm hemmed in on both sides, caught between the slippery doorknob and the even slipperier Davis Darwin.

He strolls across the grass, no longer in the slightest hurry. We both know he has me trapped. "Long time, no see," he says.

"It's been a year," I say. He comes back every Destination Day and, one way or another, manages to corner me.

Davis Darwin shrugs this off, then traps me with his microphone. "Anything you'd like to say on the second anniversary of your dear dad's departure?"

I stare at the microphone, suddenly at a loss for words. Its furry cover reminds me of this caterpillar book we used to have. Before the asteroid threw our solar system out of whack, caterpillars would eat and eat and eat until they couldn't anymore—salami, cherry pie, you name it. Then they would spin these cocoons that would turn them into butterflies. I wish I could turn that microphone into something that would fly away, but before I can say that thought out loud, the door flies open behind me.

"Get off my property," Mom says, waving her hands at the news crew like they're a pack of pesky flies. When Davis Darwin holds his ground, her face turns as red as cherry pie. "I said, get off my property!"

"Is it really yours?" he asks as his grin turns sharp and mean. "You live here because the program has agreed to let you stay, and we both know that the program has given UNN full access to Wheelock Park *and* its inhabitants."

Mom sticks out her chin. "You can have full access to *me*, but leave my son out of this mess."

Davis Darwin keeps grinning. "So protective," he replies. "But then, I'd expect nothing less from one of—"

He's cut off by the hollow *thwack* of a front door slamming shut. His bean-shaped nostrils flare as he whips around and scans the street. Kids are pouring out of houses, clearly on their way to school, and yet Davis Darwin's ears knew *that* front door was the Primms'.

"Come on, Leopold," he says. "We've got bigger meteors to burn."

A part of me feels sort of relieved, but the rest of me just feels afraid. The girl who took our cookies is setting a dizzying pace, but Davis Darwin will catch her. He always makes his mark. Then he'll tear her apart one faulty heartstring at a time, and his trusty cameraman will document the whole sad thing.

Morbid curiosity sends me darting down the street.

"Davis Darwin," he says brashly, falling into step beside her. "And you must be Astra Primm."

Her name is Astra, like the stars. I should have guessed it would be different.

Astra sends him a sideways glance, then returns her attention to the sidewalk.

He jogs to keep up. "I was wondering," he says a little breathlessly, "if my cameraman and I could have a few minutes of your time."

Astra doesn't stop, but Davis Darwin doesn't quit.

"We just want to talk," he says, brandishing the microphone like a broadsword. "History, politics, whatever." He draws a purposeful breath. "Heck, if you want to, we could even talk about your mom."

At that Astra finally stops, and from the way his body sags, I can tell that he's relieved. He must have been running out of scare tactics, but now he's back on track. He shoves the microphone into her face and patiently waits for her to crack.

But that moment never comes. Astra grabs the microphone and chucks it over his big head. It sails over the sunscreen, clips the corner of the news van, and smashes into the road.

"Fetch," is all she says before she dusts off her hands and continues on her way, leaving Davis Darwin—now without his microphone—to stare blankly after her.

I still don't know who this girl is, but I take back every unkind thought I had about her yesterday. I only have one now: I desperately want to be her friend.

# 3

I LOSE TRACK OF ASTRA during the short walk to
school, but that's probably OK. She wasn't in the mood to
talk. When I walk into the gray building, the first thing I
have to pass is the Destination: Mars display, a platform
covered with red sand and fake-looking Martian rocks. But
the centerpiece is definitely the authentic first-gen space
suit dangling from a custom rig. It's supposed to represent
the moment the first real, live human being actually set
foot on Mars.

I stop to admire it. Even though I know Dad's captain probably left the spaceship first, a part of me likes to imagine it's Dad dangling from that rig.

The first bell rings eventually, and I head over to the office. For the past two years, ever since Dad left for Mars, I've had a standing appointment with Dr. Ainge, the school psychologist. I've tried to tell Mom I'm OK—it's not like my grades are slipping because Dad's out of the picture—but she insists that I keep going. It's easier to go than to keep fighting with her.

The office hums with energy. Ms. Cook and Mr. Flores, the principal and her assistant, are fluttering around his desk, double-checking the bouquets. Most of the tracts in the shadehouses have been set aside for food production, but the gardeners always plant several rows of purple flowers for Destination Day festivities. It looks like a garden in here.

Dr. Ainge picks that moment to poke her head out of her office. "The assembly starts in twenty, so we'll have to skip our appointment."

I let my shoulders slump. "OK." She pays less attention to you if she thinks you like to talk.

"Thanks for being a good sport." She motions toward the auditorium. "You can head to the assembly. I'll tell Mr. Rix you're here."

Mr. Rix is the fifth-grade teacher at the Eleazer Wheelock Ripley Upper and Lower School, which, of course, makes him *my* teacher. He used to teach English literature at some university in Massachusetts, but after Massachusetts got swallowed up by the Atlantic, he and his son decided to move to Minnesota. When his son was picked to join the program as an astronaut, he got to move onto the base. I've never been able to decide who got the better deal.

B Hall is strangely quiet—everyone must have headed straight to class—but as soon as I turn the corner, a dull hum starts to build. Destination Day is big, even bigger than Christmas or the Fourth of July, so there's always an assembly during school and a parade after sunset. It's this pyrotechnic thing with light sticks and fireworks, but we haven't gone since I was nine. Mom doesn't like the noise, and I don't like leaving the JICC. The last thing I want to do is miss a transmission from Dad, even if they usually only come in once a week.

On the flip side, the assembly is one of the highlights of my year; I've been an honor cadet ever since Dad left for Mars. I know they only asked me because he's a program hero, but I don't mind being a stand-in. I'm as proud of him as they are.

When I get to the auditorium, I can't help but grin. Ms. Patel, the music teacher, is herding the honor cadets, several dozen noisy students in matching purple coveralls, onto a stage draped with purple streamers. There are even purple banners swinging from the rafters overhead. As the program came together, filling the hole left behind by the government's collapse, they considered picking green, then decided maybe green was a little too cliché, so they picked purple instead. Now it's my favorite color too.

I'm still standing in the doorway when Ms. Cook and Mr. Flores hurry past me, their arms laden with purple flowers. Then Astra appears, and I do a double-take.

"Hey!" I say cheerfully. Then I remember how she slammed the door shut in my face last night.

"Hi," Astra replies. Either she's remembering too, or she just doesn't want to be here.

I motion toward the stage. "So did they invite you to be an honor cadet?" If Davis Darwin was hounding her, she must be famous enough.

"Yep," Astra replies. She's got these one-word answers down, but I'm too stubborn to give up.

"That's quite an honor," I reply, then realize how that came out. "I mean, it's *clearly* an honor, since they're called honor cadets, so I guess I should have said . . ."

I trail off awkwardly. I don't know what I should have said, and Astra doesn't throw me any bones.

Luckily Ms. Patel spots us. "Get up here, Jameson!" she says, squinting at us over her glasses. "And is that droopy-looking girl standing next to you Astra?"

Astra doesn't nod, but she doesn't shake her head either.

"Well, then I need you up here too." Ms. Patel claps seven times. "All right, people, let's do this!"

I scurry up onto the stage, grateful to have a valid reason to expend my nervous energy, and take my place in the ensemble next to Evelyn Segundo. Evelyn's older than I am, but we've both been honor cadets together for as long as I can remember. I think they asked her to join because her dad died on a spacewalk to repair a faulty rocket booster, but that just makes me wonder why they invited Astra.

"Hey, little man," Evelyn whispers as she ruffles my limp hair. I wouldn't let another fifth grader ruffle my hair like that, but Evelyn's sixteen, so I let her get away with it. "Are you ready for the show?"

"Always," I whisper back.

Before it was a school for the astronauts' offspring, Eleazer Wheelock Ripley was a school for the astronauts themselves, complete with a centrifuge and a low-grav simulator. Unfortunately they moved the centrifuge after some stupid seventh grader took it for a little spin and puked all over the controls. We lost the low-grav simulator when they needed to make room for more desks.

Now Eleazer Wheelock Ripley handles kids from preschool through twelfth grade, though the school's still pretty small. Most people have decided not to have any more kids, so each grade only has one class.

Astra's just reached the stage when Ms. Patel says, "Honor cadets, I'd like you to meet the newest member of our little brigade. Astra is going to be a part of the color guard this year." She hoists the Stars and Mars out of its stand. "Astra, your battle standard."

Astra gives the purple flag a once-over, then reluctantly takes it—and proceeds to drop it on her toes. Braxton Fitzwilliam, the only twelfth grader in the group and the only other member of this year's color guard, helps her pick it up.

"It's heavier than it looks," he says with an easygoing smile. We don't have a student body president, but if we did, it would be Braxton. "Do you think you have it now?"

Astra tests its weight. "Uh-huh."

I can't help but smile smugly. At least she seems to be immune to Braxton's overly white teeth.

While the other kids come in and fill in rows of purple seats, we honor cadets quickly assemble at the back. Then, once everyone is seated, the lights lower, the anthem rises, and we march down the narrow aisles in picture-perfect unison, with Astra in the lead. Braxton waves the Stars and Stripes like our success depends on it, and who knows? Maybe it does.

Once the anthem has been sung and the pledge has been recited, Ms. Cook steps behind the podium and asks us to sit down. We honor cadets have reserved seats in the front row, but I linger by the stairs. Next up is the showing of *Earth to Mars and Back Again*, but I never get to stay for it. Mom always cracks the side door open just before the movie starts and waves me out into the hall. She always has some weird excuse. Last year, it was that she needed help with the rutabaga harvest.

I know it's weird, but that's Mom. She's crazy protective. After Dad left for Mars, I was her only family on this planet. Like me, she was an only child, and both of her parents died before I was even born.

But a part of me still wonders why I'm not allowed to watch. It isn't like the film is inappropriate or something. Maybe she's just afraid I'll be exposed to extra germs in the closed-in auditorium.

Or maybe she's not, because this year she doesn't show.

I give her another minute, then, when the side door doesn't open, quietly slink into a seat. It feels like I'm breaking a rule, but it's a rule I want to break. A part of me can't help but grin and grip the armrests with both hands as the screen flickers to life.

The film starts with an asteroid. These kinds of stories often do, but this asteroid is different. For one thing, it's enormous—slightly smaller than Pluto—and for another, it's way out in space. A scientist spots it hurtling toward us when it's still seven *billion* miles from the edge of Neptune's orbit, and based on its trajectory, the asteroid's not supposed to come within four hundred million miles of Earth's path around the sun.

But what the scientist doesn't take into account is how close it's going to come to Jupiter's orbit.

First the asteroid zooms past Pluto, skipping Neptune and Uranus because they happen to be on the far side of the sun. Then it whizzes through the gap between Saturn and Jupiter. But it's much closer to the latter, and as the asteroid buzzes past, Jupiter literally wobbles, pulled for an interstellar instant by the asteroid's gravity.

Jupiter's wobble makes the inner planets wobble too, but pint-sized Mercury, caught in a cosmic tug-of-war between the sun and Jupiter, can't take the sudden pull. It skitters off into deep space, but not before crossing paths with Venus and pulling it slightly out of orbit. Then Venus' gravity pulls us, and our gravity pulls Mars, and now we can't stop spiraling closer and closer to the sun. Trapped in an awful cosmic dance that, give or take ten thousand years, will turn us into shish kebabs.

That was a lifetime ago, nine months before I came along, but I know what happened next. Everyone knows what happened next. Temperatures skyrocketed, the Great Plains shriveled up and morphed into the Great Waste, and the North Pole began to thaw—in the middle of December. Since the Antarctic ice sheet also lost half of its volume, the oceans rose by ninety feet. No one can say for sure, but the program estimates 49 percent of Earth's inhabitants died in the first year alone.

Everyone shifts uncomfortably as the film sums up those months with a depressing news montage. All the anchors are from random towns like Racine and Missoula, towns that didn't get destroyed by the ocean or the desert. They cover water rescues and water shortages, Midwestern monsoons and category-six tornadoes. All of which seem normal to me, and yet I get the impression that the anchors are alarmed, not sure how to deal.

I'm so caught up in the film that, when a brilliant bar of light suddenly spreads across the screen, I scowl over my shoulder at what's causing the disturbance. That's when I spot Mom. The side door is wide open, and her hands are on her hips. I know I'm in trouble even before she crooks a finger.

Ignoring the sympathetic looks the honor cadets are sending me, I slowly ooze out of my seat and make my way toward the side door. I can feel everyone's eyes tracking my progress up the aisle.

As soon as I reach her, Mom lets the door swing shut. Somehow her gaze feels heavier than my two hundred schoolmates'.

"We could really use your help transplanting soybean starts," she says.

I don't meet her eyes. "All right."

"I'm sorry I was late. I had a meeting with Juwan, and you know how he likes to talk."

"It's fine," I say warily. I don't want to talk about her long-winded assistant or what they do at the shadehouses. I just want to know when she's going to lose it.

Mom looks me up and down, then tips her head toward the foyer. I fall into step beside her without a second thought.

"Well, what did you think?"

Is this a diversionary tactic? "What did I think of *what*?" I ask.

She tips her head back toward the door. *"Earth to Mars and Back Again."*

"Oh." I lick my lips. What does she want me to say? That I knew she wouldn't want me to watch? "It was . . . educational."

Mom lowers her gaze. Finally I realize that she's as nervous as I am. "Was there anything about it you found, I don't know, disturbing?"

I crinkle my nose. How am I supposed to answer *that*? "The news footage was kind of sad. Kind of scary but mostly sad."

"Is that as far as you got?"

I think about it. "Yeah, I guess."

Mom's thin shoulders sag. I can tell that she's relieved. "It *was* sad. And *really* scary." She wraps an arm around my shoulders. "I'm kind of glad you weren't born yet."

I let myself relax a little. "So you're not upset?" I ask. Maybe she really is concerned about the germs, not the movie.

"No, I'm not upset," she says. "I was just thinking about Dad."

I can certainly relate to that. "I know it must be hard for you to be away from him," I say. "But at least we know he's saving humanity, right?"

"That's exactly right," Mom says, but she doesn't sound reassured. Just tired.

\* \* \*

When we get home from the shadehouses, a food delivery truck is parked right in front of our house. The program manages our rations based on a complex formula designed to maximize our health while minimizing our consumption. The planet can't produce nearly as much food it used to, so we just have to be smarter.

"Happy Destination Day!" the driver—I think her name is Maury—says. She hands Mom our ration box.

Mom smiles tiredly. "Yes, happy Destination Day."

Maury sets her sights on me. "Are you pumped up for the parade?"

I send Mom a sideways glance. She tends to get uncomfortable when people mention the parade (or Destination Day in general), but she's managing to keep her cool. I decide to follow suit.

"No, I think we'll just stay home and play Monopoly or something."

Mom visibly relaxes.

I ask Maury the same question: "Are you pumped up for the parade?"

Her eyes light up like fireworks. "You'd better believe it," she replies. "I wouldn't miss it for the world—or any other world either!"

While Maury laughs at her own joke, Mom directs me toward the door. "Thanks for the ration box," she says.

This is clearly a dismissal, but Maury doesn't seem to notice—or if she does, she doesn't care. "No problem," she replies, waving enthusiastically. As she clomps back down the driveway, Maury adds over her shoulder, "I'll light a shooting star for you!"

I have no idea how she can light a shooting star, but it still sounds magical. *Hey, thanks!* I want to yell back, but before I can get the words out, Mom drags me into the house.

"Let's get these rations put away."

I unzip my solar jack and let it tumble to the floor. "You could have let me tell her thanks."

"Please don't leave that there," Mom says, nodding toward my solar jack. "And if I was rude, I'm sorry."

I don't believe that for a second—Mom's never been the biggest fan of these Destination Days—but the argument's not worth it. Sighing, I pick up my solar jack, then follow her into the kitchen.

Mom turns on the news—Hester Dibble is still on—and starts unpacking apricots. Fresh fruit may be a luxury, but there always seems to be enough news to go around. It must have been a slow news day, because Hester Dibble's droning on about the Magellan Six *again*. I know they only died a handful of months ago, but that woman refuses to stop talking about them.

"—and Britannia Primm, the ill-fated mission leader," Hester Dibble is saying, "all of whom have been awarded posthumous Medals of Honor for their willingness to go to Mars and, obviously, lay down their lives. Dr. Primm's whole team was killed when an asteroid attractor inadvertently guided an asteroid to the sub-Olympian plain the Magellan Six were scouting."

When Dr. Primm's official pic suddenly appears on the wall screen, I do a double-take. There's no mistaking the slim woman with the wiry black hair. If Astra ever smiled, that's exactly what she'd look like.

Now I know why they asked Astra to be an honor cadet. Her mom is one of the Magellan Six.

"Jameson?" Mom asks, but her voice sounds fuzzy and far away. I'm surprised when she touches me. "Jameson, you should sit down. You look like you're going to faint."

She guides me over to a barstool, her hands dripping with yellow juice. My shoulders are now sticky, but I only notice vaguely. Astra's mom is really dead.

"Despite this major setback," Hester Dibble continues, "the *Juan Ponce de León* is still scheduled to take off as planned . . ."

"Jameson, what's wrong?" Mom asks as she checks my eyes, my ears, my throat. When she doesn't find anything wrong with any of these body parts, she tries to poke my stomach. At least that gives me a reason to bat her hands away.

"I'm fine," I say through gritted teeth. "It was just something she said."

Mom looks around the kitchen as if she's searching for someone. By the time her eyes land on the wall screen, Hester Dibble has moved on.

"The family that moved in across the street," I say softly. "I think the mom died on Mars."

Mom draws a shaky breath, and I can tell she's trying not to lose it. I know exactly how she feels. When someone you love is off-planet, the threat is always there.

"Oh, Jamie," she replies, pulling me into a hug. I think I'm too old for hugs, but Mom says you never outgrow them. "Want to talk about it?"

"No."

She pats my shoulder absently. "I should have made more cookies."

While Mom beats herself up, I slither out of her grip and head directly to my room. I've got to check the JICC, to see if Dad sent a transmission. Everything was fine last week, but Mars is a dangerous place. You never know when that might change.

"Jameson!" Mom calls after me, but I'm already long gone.

My door closes behind me with a satisfying thump. I sag against it for a moment, then set my sights on the JICC. Dad and I started building it the day after he found out he'd be on the *Amerigo Vespucci*. First we assembled the antenna (including a reflector dish that was as big as our whole house), mounted it in the backyard, and tuned the coil to the resonant frequency of the emitter. Then we attached a superhet to stabilize incoming frequencies, which would in turn allow the JICC to produce high-quality audio-visual transmissions. *Then* we tuned the antenna to this more stable frequency.

It took Dad a while to decide how to power it, so for the next few months the JICC just sat there, baking under the poisonous sun. The emitter's power source needed to be isolated from the antenna's so power couldn't flow between them and potentially fry our equipment—not to mention us. We ended up building a self-tuning resonator for the emitter and a high-voltage relay for the antenna.

I didn't understand either, but Dad seemed to think they were important. And the high-voltage relay does look pretty amazing. It reminds me of a giant torus, though Mom thinks it looks like a doughnut. When I asked her what a doughnut was, she just sighed and shook her head.

I sink into my desk chair and frantically jiggle the mouse. For the three seconds it takes the monitor to come back to life, I'm wishing, hoping, praying for a new message from Dad. Though it's only been six days, someone must have heard my prayer, because the message bar is blinking as soon as it comes into focus: *1 NEW TRANSMISSION.*

I let the relief sink in, then swiftly type in *DOWNLOAD.* I can't help but grin when Dad's familiar face pops up. He looks kind of tired, and there's a dirt smudge on his cheek, but otherwise he seems all right.

"Hey, kid," he says with a half-smile as he wipes some kind of gunk off his hands. "It's day seven thirty-one, but I'm afraid I can't talk long. We're still trying to refurbish this one asteroid attractor that's been broken for months, so they keep pulling us away to help maintenance with the repairs."

Dad doesn't mention the Magellan Six by name, but then, he doesn't have to. As Hester Dibble just mentioned, their accident was *caused* by an asteroid attractor. There are tons of useful gases frozen in Mars' thick crust, so astronauts use tractor beams to lure rogue asteroids to the surface. The collisions create heat, and the gases unfreeze on their own. Instant oxygenation.

But playing down what happened—and the danger of what he's doing—is just how Dad deals with pressure. He's always been the sort to keep his problems to himself.

"To be honest, I'm fed up with asteroid attractors," Dad goes on. "There must be a better way to oxygenate the atmosphere." He cocks his head to the side as if to catch a passing thought. "Maybe you'll invent the tech that ends up replacing them. I certainly wouldn't put it past the smartest kid in the solar system."

I smile at the thought of inventing something useful, something Dad would really like. He starts to smile too, but then he yawns and rubs his jaw, smearing the dirt smudge on his cheek. I want to reach into the monitor and wipe it off for him, but he's millions of miles away—35, to be exact—so that's impossible, of course.

"Listen to your mother," Dad goes on. "I know she can be difficult—heaven knows she can be difficult—but she's still your mom. She only wants what's best for you. And that goes for me too. We may be on two different planets, but we're still on the same team." He glances at something to his left, then returns his attention to the camera. "Well, I guess I'd better go. We're getting ready to make another salvage run. Did you know we're still harvesting parts from that unmanned cargo ship that crashed a year or two ago? We're lucky that it was unmanned." For some reason, he won't meet my gaze as he reaches for the kill switch. "Mars to Jameson."

The monitor goes black.

"Earth to Dad," I whisper back, letting out a held-in breath. Dad is fine. He's more than fine. Just because Dr. Primm died doesn't mean he's going to die too.

I'm still trying to relax when I catch a glimpse of Astra. I feel bad for her at first, but it doesn't look like she's feeling sorry for herself. She's sneaking out her window and getting her bike from the garage.

# 4

I ASSUME THAT ASTRA'S headed down to the parade on Main Street, since that's what everyone—present company excluded—does on Destination Day. But if that's where she's headed, why would she need to sneak out? There's no way Mr. Primm is as paranoid as Mom. And she doesn't come back until almost 10:15, long after the last float would have trundled down Main Street.

Now I'm *very* curious. The next night, she sneaks out at exactly the same time. In fact, she sneaks out every night between 8:50 and 9:10 for the rest of the week, and I can't help but take notes.

For the first few nights, she comes back at different times—10:18, 10:43, and 9:57 by my watch—but on Thursday and Friday, she comes back at 10:01 and 10:02, respectively. The simplest explanation is that she spent those first few nights exploring her new territory before settling on a favorite haunt, but of course, that's pure speculation.

If I want to know for sure, I'm going to have to follow her.

Circumventing Mom is going to be the tricky part, but at least I have a plan. After she makes tofu tacos—a Saturday tradition and one of my favorite meals—I'll push my food around my plate and generally look miserable. When she asks why I'm not eating, I'll tell her I'm not feeling well, and she'll excuse me to my room. Then I'll just have to wait around until she heads into the bathroom for her weekly bubble bath—another Saturday tradition—at which point I'll make my escape.

The plan goes off without a hitch—until Mom is too lost in thought to notice my stirring performance.

"So I've been thinking," she says slowly, "about the Primms across the street."

I nearly drop my tofu taco. The Primms are the last people I want to talk about right now.

"What if we invited them over for dinner sometime soon? We could pool our ration boxes, find a way to make it work." She gazes off into the distance like she's looking at their house, but the wall is in the way. "The daughter seems like a nice girl. I'm sure you two will be great friends."

I blow my nose to hide my snort. Astra *doesn't* seem like a nice girl, but Mom is right about one thing—I *do* want to be her friend. But not because anyone forced us.

I start to take a bite, then remember I'm not hungry— or I'm not supposed to be. My stomach growls in protest as I set my food back down. Hunger strikes are extra hard when tofu tacos are involved.

At least that catches Mom's attention. "What's the matter? Are you sick? I thought you loved tofu tacos."

*Finally.* "Yeah, I think I'm sick."

"Then you should go and rest," Mom says. "I can take care of the dishes."

I narrow my eyes. "I don't have to scrape the plates?"

"Not if you aren't feeling well." She returns her attention to her food. "Just do yours before you go."

She doesn't have to tell me twice. I make a beeline for the kitchen and am about to scrape my dinner into the recycler when it occurs to me that I can hide my food instead. Then I can come back for it later. After making sure that Mom's still gazing off into the distance, I wrap up my taco and tuck it deep into the pantry, behind the sugar canister. There's no way she'll look back there.

"Good night," I half say, half slur, shuffling past her like a zombie.

As soon as I'm out of sight, I make a beeline for my room. There are no transmissions waiting for me, but for once I'm not upset. After wedging my desk chair between the doorknob and the wall, I pull on Dad's old Astros hat and hunker down below my window with Dad's field glasses in my lap. If Astra keeps to the same pattern, she won't show for another ninety minutes, but I like to plan ahead.

I recite the periodic table in my head, but when I run out of elements, I set my sights on Armstrong Street. The Cooper twins are in the middle of another rousing game of hide-and-seek, but tonight Abbott Nash is playing with a bunch of toy hovercars. They don't actually hover, but Abbott doesn't seem to care. He's floating them around his driveway, sometimes higher, sometimes lower. Though real hovercars hover at a constant height, I guess rules don't apply when you're playing make-believe.

I don't realize I've drifted off until the roar of water rushing through the pipes in the bathroom snaps me awake again. Nervously I scan the street. The Cooper twins have disappeared, but Abbott's still playing in his driveway. And Astra's turquoise bike is still poking out of her garage. I sag back against my desk, relieved. At least I didn't blow my chance.

To keep myself awake, I decide to send a new transmission. After waking up the JICC, I type in *UPLOAD* with my index finger. The camera is built in, so I know it's ready to go as soon as my goofy face pops up on the monitor.

"Hey, Dad," I say cheerfully, more cheerfully than I feel. I glance at the calendar I use to keep track of the days that he's been gone. "It's day seven thirty-six, and I'm just chilling. In my room. I already did my homework. I'm *not* spying on the neighbors."

I pause and let myself daydream about Dad's response: *Way to do your homework, kid. Way to not spy on the neighbors.* The JICC is super great, but it would be even greater if we could have *real* conversations. Not that the delay, which can last up to twenty minutes, would ever make that possible.

"Anyway," I say, "I'm not going to be able to chat for very long, since I have something to do later."

I know I'm treading closer to unsafe territory, but it's not like Dad can ground me or even get very upset. He probably did way worse when he was my age. Back when we thought Earth had forever and kids could just be kids. Also, I know for a fact that he never sends Mom messages, so it's not like he can squeal.

"If you were still around, I'd ask you about this . . . girl." I realize how that must sound and race to add, "It's not like that, so stop smiling. I just want to be her friend, mostly because she knows how to deal with that bothersome reporter who's always sniffing around."

I'm about to describe how Davis Darwin looked when his favorite microphone smashed into a thousand pieces when Mom knocks on my door, then forces it in from the outside. The door bonks into the desk chair, sending it spinning into the wall. I guess I don't know how to wedge it.

"What's your chair doing over here?" Mom asks as she pokes her head into the room. Her wet hair is dangling around her face, and she's wearing Dad's old robe, like she just hopped out of the tub. "And who are you talking to?"

I motion casually toward the JICC. "Just sending a transmission," I reply. Then I get a weird idea. "Do you want to . . . tell Dad hi?"

Mom never sends Dad messages. She always has some dumb excuse—*It's too early. It's too late. I don't have my makeup on.*—but I think she resents the JICC and how much time I spend on it.

Tonight she doesn't even bother with the flimsy explanations. "I'd better not," she says, pulling the door closed on her heels.

My throat gets tight and itchy, like I'm on the verge of tears. I hold my breath and count to ten. A sob is one transmission I don't want to send to Mars. But I can't hold my breath forever, so instead of passing out, I murmur, "Earth to Dad," hit the *SEND* button, and turn off the monitor.

I'm still staring at the screen when a flash catches my eye and I remember why I'm here. It's exactly 8:50, and Astra is sneaking out.

I adjust my Astros hat and slip out into the hall. "September Moon" is blaring from the iPod Mom has had for years, so I think it's safe to say that she got back into the tub. After her run-in with the JICC, she probably won't come out again tonight. Maybe it's not a bad thing that she walked in on that transmission.

After easing my door closed, I creep down the darkened hall and let myself out the side door. Mom's standard-issue

Ford Light-Year takes up most of the garage, so I have to tiptoe around it to review my transportation options. I could take the lime-green bike Dad got me for my fifth birthday, but I haven't ridden it since I nearly cracked my skull open trying to climb onto the seat. I guess that leaves me with the hoverboard, which, unlike Abbott's hovercars, actually hovers.

The hoverboard whirs enthusiastically as I drag it out of its corner. After the sun went ballistic, a bunch of companies invested in solar-powered transportation, but the program only purchased the super techy, high-end stuff—until they decided to absorb those companies. I got this hoverboard from them, but despite the high-end label, I can't stop tinkering with it. This sucker can now hold a charge for almost four and a half months.

I can't help but wince as I turn on the hoverboard. It's not as loud as Mom's Light-Year, but it might still be loud enough to drown out "September Moon." With any luck, I'll be long gone before Mom bothers to investigate. Of course, that's assuming I don't fall flat on my face.

After saying a quick prayer to whoever might be listening, I climb onto the hoverboard and take off after Astra. I wobble back and forth at first, but I do manage to stay upright. Astra comes into view at the end of Armstrong Street.

At first I hang back, *way* back, but when Astra doesn't check behind her, I finally let myself relax. The slightly cooler air reminds me of walking to school back when they tried to flip everyone's sleep cycles and keep us awake during the night. As it turns out, people need sunlight, even if it's mostly toxic. After the suicide rate tripled, they went back to the old schedule, but I still miss being outside in the middle of the night, when the bruised sky and twinkling stars let me pretend I was on Mars.

Astra navigates Wheelock Park expertly, pausing only once to let another Light-Year pass. It isn't super late, and yet I'm still surprised when she doesn't try to hide. The Light-Year ignores her, but as we get closer to the gate, I feel my hands start to sweat. Wheelock Park is watched over by a squat gray guardhouse, and I've heard that the guard, a crotchety old man named Branislav, won't let you through the gate without a parent's permission.

When the guardhouse comes into view, I seriously consider turning back. Astra's only lived here for the past five or six days, so she can't know about Branislav. She's going to get herself arrested. I cup both hands around my mouth and am about to stage-whisper a warning when she veers off to the left.

Against my better judgment, I veer off to follow her.

At the edge of the Brandts' yard, Astra checks over her shoulder. I freeze in the middle of the sidewalk and rack my brains for a good reason to be shadowing her movements. But instead of confronting me, she hops nimbly off her bike and ducks behind a nearby hedge.

I wait for her to come back out, but when I count to 306 and she still hasn't reappeared, I have no choice but to investigate. I walk my hoverboard across the street and press my back against the hedge. Dried twigs scrape my neck and get tangled in my hair, but when I finally muster the courage to sneak a peek around the corner, the other side is strangely empty—except for Astra's bike.

As my pulse decelerates, I try to decide if I'm more worried or relieved. Either Astra teleported, or there's a hidden door nearby.

I ditch my hoverboard next to her bike and get down on my hands and knees. It doesn't take long to find the chain-link gate on the north side of the yard, directly behind a hacked-out recess in the sickly hedge.

The dirt is warm under my hands as I scurry through the gate. The creaky latch catches on my collar, but I manage to ignore it. I've let Astra get too far ahead. If I don't catch up to her soon, there's a good chance that I'll lose her.

Once I emerge from the Brandts' hedge, I brush off my hands and knees, though I don't stand up just yet. I've emerged onto Main Street, which is wider and more brightly lit than the streets in Wheelock Park, so I'm happy to survey the scene from the safety of the shadows.

The guardhouse is off to my right now. Across from it is the school. I can see Mr. Rix's window and one corner of the playground, but there's still no sign of Astra. Not that I find that surprising. Who sneaks out to go to *school*? Not even I'm that desperate.

That leaves the rest of Main Street, a picture-perfect boulevard that includes a bank, a Laundromat, and even an ice cream shop. Of course, the whole thing's a facade for the *real* business that takes place on Main Street: security, surveillance, and bureaucracy. As soon as you walk into the bank, the automated tellers ask for your name, birth date, and tag number so they can buzz you back to the appropriate department, and the Laundromat is the ground floor of the observation tower. It looms over the landscape like a dark gray obelisk, the closest thing we have to a mountain. It can't have anything to do with Astra.

But as soon as I think that, I spot her.

She could have suction cups for hands as easily as she scales the building. It takes her another minute to reach the top of the wall, and then, for two vulnerable seconds, she slides into the moonlight, a black and blue smudge against the blacker and bluer sky. But I'd know that Mickey Mouse hair anywhere.

My pulse pounds in my ears as I creep across the street. She must have used the alley directly across from the Brandts' gate, but it's barely more than an inlet and as dark as a black hole. If I hadn't just watched her climb out of those menacing shadows, I might have missed it altogether.

After drawing a deep breath, I plunge into the alley. It's so dark in here that my eyes need time to adjust, but then I spot the huge recycler at the back of the alley—and the thick black ladder mounted to an outer wall. With slightly trembling hands, I test the lowest rung. It's a little grimy, but it seems solid enough. As long as I maintain three points of contact, I should be just fine.

Should be.

I only make it up five rungs before I start to hyperventilate. My hands are hot and sweaty, and somehow I already feel like I'm scraping the stratosphere. How have I never realized that I'm deathly afraid of heights?

When I feel my fingers start to slip, I loop my arm over the rung to keep from plunging to my death—or, at the very least, my breaking. Too late, I realize my sleeve will now be coated with a thick layer of grime, which Mom is bound to notice. But if I do get in trouble for ruining my nicest shirt, at least I'll be alive.

I squeeze my eyes shut and pray. I'm on the verge of promising to always eat my brussels sprouts if I can just survive tonight when something whacks me in the face and a gruff voice says, "Grab on."

It takes me less than a second to realize the something is a rope and the gruff voice belongs to Astra.

I look heavenward. Her face is wreathed in shadow, but her teeth glisten like gems. Not that Astra's smiling—I don't think she ever does—but she did toss me a rope. I consider using it to rappel down to the ground, then decide I probably won't be any better at going down than I was at going up. Besides, it would be rude to run after she saved my life.

The rest of the climb is as tedious as it is embarrassing. Using clipped, two-word commands, she shows me how to tie the rope so she can catch me if I fall, but I still have to do the work. I've just grabbed another rung when I happen to look down and lose my footing in the process. Grunting, Astra braces herself against the top of the wall, but she doesn't bite my head off. Maybe she's nicer than I thought.

Finally my forehead pokes above the top of the building, then my eyes, then my nostrils. I wrap both arms around the ledge and half slither, half crawl onto the corner of the roof.

"Did I—make it?" I ask between noisy gasps for breath.

"More or less," Astra replies, wriggling out of her end of the rope.

I shuck the rope off too and scramble away from the edge. I've lived on the base for most of my natural life, but I've never seen it quite like this, spread out below me like a map. Wheelock Park reminds me of a LEGO village from up here, with its rows of matching houses set on squares of matching yards. The school looks more substantial, but it's still dwarfed by the complex several miles to the east, which stretches forever. That's where the president and the scientists who run the program live. I can see the backlit outlines of shadehouses to the north and the dull glow of Murphyville, our sister city, to the south. The rest is plain, old desert sand, an unforgiving ocean of it. It's what the whole world will be once the sun has its way with us.

I'm still gawking at the view when Astra chucks the rope aside and makes her way across the roof. I couldn't see it from below, but she's got a whole hangout up here complete with lights, two broken chairs, a holovid for watching stuff, and a bunch of crates for tables.

I can't help but gape in wonder. "Did you drag all this stuff up here?" I had a hard enough time getting myself up that dumb ladder.

Grudgingly she shakes her head. "Most of it was here already. I just brought the holovid."

I crinkle my nose. "Why?" Wall screens have better resolution.

Astra sinks into the less broken of the two broken chairs. "I don't know. To get away?"

I think I get what she means. If UNN kept sharing pics of my dead mom and her crew, I'd want to escape too. "I'm sorry about your mom."

Astra laughs, not very nicely. "You and every other Ripley."

I wince despite myself. "At least she lived a good life. A worthwhile life, you know?"

"I thought she was living a worthwhile life when she was just my mom."

This response surprises me. Who wouldn't want to have a program hero for a parent? "You didn't want her to go to Mars?"

"Did I want her to hitch a ride to some faraway planet in a tin can powered by a string of nuclear explosions? I'm gonna mark that as a no."

"But it's for the greater good."

"Yeah, well, we'll see how you feel when it's *your* dad who gets smooshed by a wayward asteroid."

I open my mouth to answer, then snap it shut again. Tears are pooling in my eyes, so even if I tried to speak, I would probably just blubber.

Astra lowers her gaze. "I'm sorry," she mumbles, grabbing a box of Nilla Wafers and stuffing a handful into her mouth. "Don't listen to a word I say." Around a mouthful of pale crumbs, she adds, "After all, I'm just the daughter of the program's latest hero."

She says it so miserably that I mostly forgive her. When she tips the box toward me, I forgive her all the way. I dig out a Nilla Wafer, then sit down on a nearby crate and tip my head back toward the sky. We're high enough above the ground that the streetlamps don't interfere, so I can see the Little Dipper and even Andromeda, our galaxy's next-door neighbor.

Before Dad left for Mars, we would stargaze from our roof, and he would tell me that, even if our Earth was the only inhabitable planet in the entire Milky Way, there was probably an Earth somewhere in Andromeda. And if there was an Earth somewhere in Andromeda, there was probably an Earth somewhere in every galaxy, which meant there were more worlds like ours than we could ever even count. Now that he's up there too, that thought makes me feel less lonely.

"It's nice up here," I finally say. "It makes me feel closer to . . . everything."

Astra sniffs too loudly. "Well, don't think that you can climb up here whenever you feel like it. This is *my* quiet place, not yours."

"Don't worry," I reply. "I *can't* climb up here without you."

I can't say for sure, but it looks like one corner of her mouth twitches like she's trying not to laugh—or, at the very least, smile.

We sit in silence for a while, until Astra finally asks, "Do you know what the worst part is?"

About having a dead mom? Solemnly I shake my head. I can think of lots of worsts, but the last thing I want to do is put my words into her mouth.

"The worst part is that I'll never get to see my mom again. They say it's 'a waste of resources'"—she makes air quotes with her fingers—"to ship a body home, so they just buried her up there."

She motions toward the sky and the faintly reddish star that isn't actually a star, then wraps her arms around her knees. "I just wish I'd been there when they lowered her into the ground. Then I'd know for sure that it was over—and that I'd been there for her."

As soon as she says it, an idea pops into my head. She may not have been there, but I know someone who was.

# 5

BY THE TIME I GET HOME, I'm too tired to do more than throw myself onto my bed, so as soon as I wake up, I dive headlong for my desk chair. If I can send Dad a new message before he answers the old one, I can ask him for more information about the Magellan Six, and especially Dr. Primm.

Excitement courses through my veins as I fire up the JICC—until I notice that the message bar is already blinking. *1 NEW TRANSMISSION*, it declares.

Until today those blinking words have never disappointed me. Reluctantly I type in *DOWNLOAD*, and Dad's smiling face appears. He's sitting farther back this time, so I can see most of the pod and his mud-splattered fatigues.

"It's day seven thirty-seven, and now that we've finished repairing that faulty asteroid attractor, it's back to the spud harvest. Have I told you they turn pink when you plant them in this dirt? It makes them look like giant turnips, but they taste a lot better."

Even though I'm disappointed, I can't help but laugh. Dad's made this joke before, but somehow it never gets old.

Dad leans back in his seat. "I wish you could see the stars up here, Jameson. The greenhouses are located on the far end of the colony, so when you're out there working, you have an uninterrupted view."

It's strange to think that greenhouses have any kind of view. I guess they serve the same function as the shadehouses do here—to grow food in a locale it wouldn't otherwise grow in—but the shadehouses are dark, almost suffocating structures mostly buried in the ground. They're not really the best places to lie back and look at the stars.

"I don't know this sky as well as I know ours," Dad says, "but I've picked out the Southern Cross, and did you know that you can see Orion from the southern hemisphere too? It's upside down, but it's Orion. Of course, if you ask Javier, he'll say it's right-side up, but he also thinks soccer is superior to football."

Javier Bartolomé, the program's chief hydrologist, is the most patriotic person on Dad's planet or ours. He's originally from South America, but his former country, a long, skinny place called Chile, is mostly underwater now. The part that isn't underwater is a craggy mess of mountains that soar to twenty thousand feet before they drop into the sea. *Los dientes de Dios*, Javier called them. "God's teeth."

"Those are the only ones I know by name, but there's this other constellation that reminds me of a dog." Dad pulls a pen out of his pocket and grabs a nearby scrap of paper—it looks like something he ripped out of a log—then punches out the pattern and holds it up for me to see. "Maybe you could look it up for us?"

I copy it down in the notebook I keep next to the JICC for this very situation. It does look like a dog—a sickly, skeletal dog. I definitely plan to look it up.

Dad lowers the scrap of paper. "Well, I'd better get back to it, but it's been great to talk to you." He reaches for the camera's kill switch as he murmurs, "Mars to Jameson."

The monitor goes dark, but I'm too jazzed to turn it off. Dad's talk of constellations jarred a long-embedded memory, and now it's bouncing around inside my skull, waiting for my consciousness to catch it. Then it does—the telescope.

Back in our stargazing days, Dad and I hit a brick wall. We'd gone as far as we could go with our unaided eyes, but we wanted to keep going, so we went to the commissary and picked up a telescope. Even though the one we got was nowhere near as awesome as the program's ELT (which stands for—I'm not even kidding—Extremely Large Telescope), it was good enough for us.

Every night for weeks on end, we dragged it up onto the roof as soon as we ran out of daylight and could no longer work on the JICC. But after Dad got on that spaceship, Mom laid down some ground rules—literally. She said I was too young to climb onto the roof all by myself, so she took the telescope away.

It's probably still in her closet. That's where Mom puts all the things she doesn't want me to play with, like Dad's old snow globe collection and the partially broken flash drive that has their wedding album. But she's never *said* I can't go into her closet, and it isn't like I'm going to take something that isn't mine.

After making sure that Mom is busy doing what moms do, I tiptoe across the hall and ease her door shut on my heels. The blackout drapes are drawn, but the window stills glows faintly, so I can just make out the bed and the dresser across from it. The closet is in the back corner, as far from the door as you can get. I guess I'll have to take this slow.

I take each step carefully, only lowering my weight onto the ball of each foot once I'm certain that the floorboard isn't going to complain. But Mom must have bionic ears, because I'm still six feet away when the door behind me crashes open and she blurts, "What are you doing in here?"

"Nothing," I say automatically. "I'm not doing anything."

"Well, you must be doing *something*." Her eyes flicker toward the closet, and the blood drains from her cheeks. "You didn't go in there, did you?"

I shake my head, and she relaxes. But her reaction makes me wary. What could she possibly be hiding in her tiny walk-in closet?

She knots her arms across her waist. "Well, did you want something?" she asks.

"Just the telescope," I peep. Thank goodness my voice didn't crack. "I thought I'd lend it to Astra."

Mom lets her arms fall to her sides, and now it's my turn to relax. "That's very thoughtful," she replies, then disappears into her closet. She pushes the door shut behind her with an easy-to-interpret whack.

I shift my weight from foot to foot while I wait for her to come back out and wonder what she might be hiding. My birthday's coming up in May, so maybe she's been stashing presents in the back of her closet.

Or maybe she chucked the telescope and thought that I'd never find out.

"Is this it?" Mom replies when she comes back a minute later, holding out a leather case that looks like it survived a war.

I nearly fall flat on my face. She didn't chuck it after all.

"That's it," I half say, half breathe as I relieve her of her burden. When I tug open the zipper, the telescope's barrel fairly gleams.

Mom ruffles my hair, then gently smooths my cowlick down. "You're a good boy, Jameson. And an even better friend."

Her compliment glows in my chest as I zip the case back up and haul it over to my room. I suck deep breaths in through my nose and push them back out through my mouth, trying not to hyperventilate. If going over to Astra's was hard when I had Mom leading the way, going over there alone might be close to impossible.

Finally I decide that if I'm going to do it, I have to just do it. Without another thought, I launch myself out of my room and rocket through the front door. Mom hollers after me, but I don't stop, don't slow down. If she wants to know where I'm going, she can just look out the window.

As I dash across the grass, a flash of plaid catches my eye. When I look down, I realize that I'm still in my pajamas—and that I didn't grab my solar jack. That must have been what Mom was trying to tell me as I left. I shudder to a halt, halfway between my starting point and my destination. I should probably go back—it would be safer to go back—but I can't lose my nerve now.

I race up Astra's driveway to her slightly covered porch. Still, the morning sun is doing a number on my neck. Luckily the door swings open almost as soon as I knock, but this time it's Mr. Primm. He takes one look at me and instantly snaps to attention.

"Sorry," I mumble, glancing down at my pajamas. "I must have forgotten to get dressed."

"Where's your solar jack?" he asks. At the same time, a familiar voice hollers from across the street, "Jameson, you'll catch your death!"

I pretend not to hear Mom, though I do slide forward a step, into the sliver of shade under the porch's overhang. I may be an idiot, but I'm not completely suicidal.

"Come in," Mr. Primm says as he waves me into the house. Before he shuts the door, he cups a hand around his mouth and shouts, "You have nothing to fear! We're bringing him in as we speak!"

He must think I'm a fugitive. Still, I accept the invitation, sneaking a peek over my shoulder as I squirm into the house. Mom's lips are pressed into a line, but instead of shouting more advice, she spins around and shuts the door.

Mr. Primm pats me on the back. "I'm sure she won't stay mad for long."

"That's because you don't know her."

Mr. Primm half grins, half winces, like he can't quite decide whether I'm joking or not. I don't have the heart to tell him I sincerely wish I were.

"I'm Carl Primm," he says, even though I already know. "What can I help you with?"

I adjust my grip on the cumbersome case. "I just had something for Astra." I try to wrestle it into his arms. "Do you think you could give it to her?"

He folds his arms across his chest and tilts his head toward the kitchen. "Give it to her yourself," he says with an exaggerated wink.

I don't know how I didn't notice, but Astra has appeared in the archway. I fiddle with my sleeve self-consciously—if I felt underdressed before, I feel almost naked now—but she doesn't seem to care, just pads across the entryway and jerks the case out of my arms. She unzips it far enough to expose the insignia on the telescope's barrel, then hastily zips it back up.

"Where'd you get this?" she demands.

"From the commissary," I reply. "Well, actually, from my mom's closet. But my dad got it from the commissary before he left for Mars." The commissary's where you go if you need anything or everything. It's like a mega megastore. "I thought you might like to borrow it, take it up on the roof."

Astra gives an almost imperceptible shake of her head, her eyes sliding toward her dad. I feel the heat crawl up my neck and pray that he doesn't take note. Of course she hasn't told him. She doesn't plan to.

"You know, so you can feel a closer to your . . . Mars."

I meant to say "your mom," but the last word wouldn't come out. But from the way Astra's smirk slowly morphs into a grin, I can tell that she gets it.

Mr. Primm pats me on the back again. *"Thank you,"* he says. "It's been a long time since I've seen my daughter smile."

"It's a nice smile," I say before I remember who I'm talking to.

He doesn't seem to mind, just throws his head back and laughs. "Would you like to stay for lunch?"

I almost trip over my feet. I wasn't expecting an invite. "Oh no, that's all right," I say. "I should probably get back."

Mr. Primm nods knowingly, then pulls out a spare solar jack and calmly offers it to me. "For the return trip," he replies.

"Won't you guys need it?" I ask.

He considers that, then shrugs. "I guess you'll have to bring it back the next time you drop by," he says with another exaggerated wink.

# 6

I WORRY ABOUT THAT SOLAR JACK for the rest of the afternoon. Mr. Primm probably assumed he was doing me a favor, but I don't know the procedure for returning borrowed items. I've never had a friend I could borrow items from. Should I make a special trip or wait for some kind of invite? If I have to wait for Astra, I could be waiting a *long* time.

I know I'll see her on the way to school, so after inhaling my breakfast bright and early the next morning,

I grab the extra solar jack and keep watch from the window. She still hasn't shown her face by the time I have to leave, so I have no choice but to carry it to school.

By the time I get to school, I'm sweating like I have the flu, so I rip off my solar jack and wad it up under one arm. I look for Astra in the places I would go—the lunchroom, the open lab, sometimes even the library—but she's nowhere to be found. At 7:58 I'm forced to admit defeat. I can't be late to my appointment with Dr. Ainge.

With another Destination Day behind us, the office has gone back to looking like an office and smelling like Mr. Flores' odiferous cologne. He claims that it's imported from one of the Polish Isles, but we've figured out the truth: His so-called supplier dumps chemicals into a vat, pours it into a nice bottle, and slaps a fancy label on it. The only things that cross the Atlantic Ocean these days are gigantic hurricanes.

My arms may be full, but my feet know where they're going. Dr. Ainge's door is the first one on the right. I'm so busy wrestling the solar jacks that I don't notice it's closed until I walk straight into it.

Mr. Flores looks up from the romance novel he keeps hidden in his desk. "Sorry, Jameson," he says, "but Dr. Ainge is with another student."

The solar jacks slide out of my arms. She can't be with another student. I've been her Monday-morning patient ever since Dad left for Mars.

Mr. Flores tips his head toward the solar jacks I'm holding. "I can take those off your hands. You must feel like a pack mule."

"What's a pack mule?" I reply. It sounds like a cargo ship, but I'm familiar with the latest models. It could be an animal. Last year Ms. Jackson taught our class about this guy named Hannibal, who transported a whole army on these things called elephants. I haven't seen an animal since our field trip to the slaughter yards.

Mr. Flores waves that off. "Never mind." It must take too long to explain.

The creak of a door opening saves me from responding. The sudden change in air pressure fans my sweaty skin, but I don't have a chance to relish it before Astra appears.

The only thing more awkward than stumbling across an almost-friend is stumbling across an almost-friend in Dr. Ainge's doorway. I stare. Astra stares. Mr. Flores leans forward in his seat.

Not knowing what else to do, I thrust the solar jack at Astra. I hope it's not too wet where my hand's been sweating on it. "Here," I say stupidly.

Astra doesn't answer, but at least she takes the solar jack before she stalks away.

"Thanks again!" I holler after her.

She raises the hand that's not clutching the solar jack, but whether it's a salute or a dismissal, I honestly can't tell.

Dr. Ainge doesn't say a word as I slip in to her office and take my usual seat, the plastic one with shock absorbers. It's comfier than the club chair and less tickly than the mohair beanbag.

For a long time, we just sit there, basking in the earthy scent of her avocado tree. Of course, her silences say more than most people's monologues, so I can imagine what she'd say if she were more talkative:

*I see that you've met Astra.*

*She moved in across the street.*

*So you've been over to her house?*

*Well, Mom wanted to make cookies.*

*Making cookies for new neighbors is a friendly thing to do.*

*Am I not usually friendly?*

The squeak of her desk chair draws me back to the real world. I wait impatiently for Dr. Ainge to say something about Astra. My answer dances on my tongue, practically begging to be blurted, but for once, she surprises me.

"You seem . . . happier," she says.

I lean back in my seat. That *wasn't* supposed to be her line. "Why do you say that?" I ask.

She motions toward the door, which has since eased itself shut. "In the waiting room, you shouted, 'Thanks again!' Correct me if I'm wrong, but wouldn't you say your tone was, well, eager?"

I would say my tone was panicked, but I know better than to substitute my impressions for Dr. Ainge's. If she's decided that I'm eager, then I'm definitely eager. Nothing will convince her otherwise.

She places both hands on her knees. "And I see that you've met Astra."

*Now* we're getting somewhere. I lean forward again, but before I can deliver my reply, she redirects the conversation one more time: "I think that you and she could learn something from each other."

I rub the back of my neck, and my sunburn sings in protest. "We could?" I ask, wincing.

Dr. Ainge plucks a dead leaf off her bonsai tree. The program usually frowns on raising non-food-bearing plants, but they overlook her office because she claims it helps her patients. I've never thought much of her potted plants one way or the other, but if she wants to delude herself, who am I to tell her any differently?

Instead of clarifying, Dr. Ainge drops the dead leaf into her recycler. "Have you ever heard of *Long-Range Communication Systems for Beginners and Non-Beginners?*"

Cautiously I shake my head.

Dr. Ainge crosses the room to the massive built-in bookcase that occupies the wall behind me. I fiddle with the mohair beanbag while she looks over the spines. It's usually my job to direct our conversations, so this is dangerously uncharted territory.

"Ah yes, here it is." She sits down in the club chair and hands me a heavy book. I can't help but wonder what she thinks I'll do with it, but luckily she reads my mind. "I'd like you to read the first couple of chapters this week."

I eye the reflector dish that's plastered across the cover. "You know that the JICC is basically a satellite, right?" I try to give her the book back. "I already know how to build one."

She refuses to take it. "Yes, but when you built the JICC, you had your father to help you. The next time you build one, you'll probably be on your own."

"Who says I'm going to build another JICC?"

Dr. Ainge holds up her hands. "The *only* thing I'm saying is that you really never know when you may need to draw on a predetermined skill set."

I narrow my eyes. "Do you know something I don't?"

"I know many somethings that you don't." She taps the cover with her pen. "But if you read *Long-Range Communication Systems,* I can guarantee you'll be ahead of me in at least one field."

* * *

The book sits at the bottom of my backpack for the rest of the day, a constant reminder of my mission, should I choose to accept it. Though lugging it around is the opposite of easy, I'm the first one out the door as soon as Mr. Rix says we can go. I don't want anyone to see it, or I might have to explain about the JICC. Mom says the other kids would want to use it all the time, so we keep it a secret. I'm so obsessed with getting home and finding somewhere to stash it that I don't notice Mom until she leans out of the Light-Year and cups her hands around her mouth.

"Isn't this a nice surprise?" she shouts.

I wouldn't call it a surprise so much as an ambush. Mom hasn't picked me up from school since I peed my pants in the first grade.

"Come on, come on," she says, waving me into the car. "We have some errands to run!"

Since when is running errands worthy of an exclamation point? Still, I don't protest, just hurry over to the Light-Year and climb into the passenger seat. Hopefully no one remembers the last time Mom picked me up from school.

"How's your sunburn?" she asks as we pull out into traffic.

"Fine," I say distractedly. I'm still thinking about that book.

Mom doesn't look convinced, but at least she lets it go. "Well, I felt bad about what happened, and it made me start to wonder if maybe you forgot your jacket because you're embarrassed by it."

I forgot my solar jack because I was in a hurry and didn't want to lose my nerve. How could I be embarrassed by a plain, old solar jack?

"I know they've come out with six or seven new models since we last got you a jacket, so I thought it was time"— she pauses for effect—"to go and get you a new one!"

I can't help but arch an eyebrow. If Mom really thinks the prospect of getting a new solar jack is going to excite me, she doesn't know me very well.

"Don't give me that look," she replies. She tucks her hair behind her ear, and I notice that she's curled the ends. "It's been a long time since we've gone to the commissary."

I glance over my shoulder. "As long as it doesn't take long." I like to look over the JICC as soon as I get home from school.

The drive to the commissary is lengthy but uneventful. Base Ripley takes up more than fifty thousand acres, and we have to stop once for a convoy and three times for the tanks that haul the program's rocket fuel out to the launch site. By the time that Mom pulls up to the commissary, the sun's already dropped behind its unimpressive gray facade.

"In and out?" I ask.

She checks her hair in the rearview. "In and out," she says as she climbs out of the car.

I cling to this promise as we cross the crowded parking lot and the automatic door sweeps open. Mom says they designed it to look like a warehouse store complete with shelves and friendly greeters, but the seven-foot autobatons that stand on both sides of the door have never made *me* feel very welcome.

I think they designed this place to look like a warehouse, period. The forklift-wide aisles are lined with metal shelving units that nearly graze the vaulted ceiling, and every aisle seems to stretch farther than the eye can see. The one good thing about this place is that, if you keep to the program's rules, you can take pretty much whatever you want. They say they charge base credits, but no one ever runs out.

As soon as we're inside, Mom makes a break for Appliances, but I grab her arm and point. "Solar jacks are over there."

"Oh right," she replies as she blinks and looks around. But then she just keeps going. "But since we're already here, I should check out the latest line of waterless dish sanitizers."

I can't remember the last time she wanted to check out *anything*, but moms are curious creatures. I don't bother to argue, just head over to the solar jacks, one aisle past the space food and a few shelving units up from the standard-issue coveralls.

The commissary's big enough that it still feels mostly empty even when the parking lot is full, but two scraggly guys are lurking in this aisle too. I pretend not to notice them as I pick through the solar jacks, including more than one that claims to have a built-in cooling system.

The shorter one ignores me back, but the taller one peeks at me, then does a double-take and stares. "Hey, do I know you?" he asks.

"I don't think so," I reply, taking an unconscious step back.

The taller man nudges his friend. "How do I know him?" he asks.

The shorter man looks up, then looks back down almost as fast. "Oh, that's James O'Malley's kid."

The taller man smacks him on the back. "See, I *knew* I knew his face!" He sends me a sideways glance. "I just wanted to say, kid—"

"Jameson!" a shrill voice cuts in.

I glance over my shoulder. Mom's standing at the far end of the aisle, hands planted on her hips. There's a line between her eyes that makes it look like she'll be trouble.

The taller man must think so too, because he shuffles back a step. "I'm sorry, ma'am," he says, concentrating on his toes. "I know you've probably taught him not to chitchat with strangers."

Mom sidles up to me. "Actually I've taught my son not to believe a word they say." She snakes an arm around my waist. "If you'll excuse us, gentlemen."

The shorter man pays us no heed, but the taller one draws a quick breath, like he's gearing up to speak. Not that Mom gives him a chance—without so much as a goodbye, she steers me toward another aisle.

It's not until we've put some distance between us and the taller man that I realize I'm shaking. I'm glad that Mom came to my rescue, because I had no idea what to say or how to say it. *This* is why I don't like going out. People are way scarier than anything on Mars.

"Are you all right?" Mom finally asks.

I start to shake my head, then change my mind at the last second. "I'm fine," I say, quaking. "It's not like they did anything."

"Did they *say* something?" Mom asks.

I consider that, then shrug. "Not really," I admit. "I just . . . don't really like . . . talking. To people I've never met."

"Fair enough," she says, shrugging. Then she sends me a sideways glance. "But what about people you *have* met?"

I narrow my eyes. "What are you talking about?"

"Oh, I just stumbled across Carl and invited him and his kids to dinner. He suggested Thursday night."

"Who's *Carl*?" I reply. I can't help but make a face.

"You know, Mr. Primm," she says. "He agreed to lend me some potatoes so I can make my gnocchi soup!"

I frown despite myself. Since when are Mom and Mr. Primm on a potato-lending basis?

Mom notices my empty arms. "Didn't you pick out a new jacket?"

I feel the heat crawl up my neck. After those scraggly guys started talking about me, I forgot about the solar jacks. "I couldn't find any I liked."

"Fair enough," she says again as she points me toward the door. "I think our mission here is done."

The way that she says it makes something click inside my head. "Did you *know* Mr. Primm would be here?"

Mom clucks her tongue dismissively. "A lady never shares her secrets."

She might as well have just said yes.

# 7

WHEN THE DOORBELL RINGS on Thursday night, I immediately pop out of my chair. "I'll answer it!" I shout as I dash out of my room. I've been looking forward to extra time with Astra, but I wish spending time with her wouldn't give Mom an opportunity to spend time with Mr. Primm. The less time they hang out, the better.

I don't hear Mom's reply, but when she's making gnocchi soup, nuclear bombs can't interrupt her. She says it's her specialty (though that may just be because potatoes grow well in shadehouses).

My socks slide on the carpet when I take the turn too sharply. At least I crash into the door instead of the corner of the coffee table.

"What was that?" Astra demands as soon as I open the door. She's wearing her solar jack, but the hood hangs loose around her neck. "It sounded like you literally smashed into the door."

I fight the urge to rub my forehead. "Would you guys like to come in?"

Mr. Primm sets down the kid he's been carrying around. With the solar jack's snug hood cinched around his/her/its face, I still can't tell whether the preschooler is a boy or a girl, but either way, he/she/it wastes no time speeding across the living room to Dad's old chess set. Mr. Primm tries to protect it, but I barely even flinch. If terrorists couldn't destroy it back when Dad was in the army, then I doubt this rug rat can.

Astra creeps into the house when she thinks no one is looking. She tilts her head this way and that, like she's never seen a house before (though it could just be she can't see past her solar jack). Finally she points her chin at the far wall and asks, "What's the deal with the scrap metal?"

I glance at the collection of twisted metal on the wall. I've gotten so accustomed to it that I barely notice anymore.

"Dad liked to hunt back in the day, but when the forests started frying and the elk started dropping dead, he decided to start hunting for bits of scrap metal instead." I squint and cross my eyes. "He tried to look for pieces that reminded him of antlers, but some of them require you to use your imagination."

Astra doesn't have a chance to answer before Mom appears in the archway. Her sweaty face is streaked with lines of grated potato, but she doesn't seem to notice.

"I didn't hear the doorbell ring," she says, taking a swipe at her forehead. She only succeeds in smearing the grated potato. "Jameson, please take their jackets."

Mr. Primm looks at the preschooler, who's now gnawing on a bishop. "We'll have to wrestle Janus for it." He unknots the hood and pulls chubby arms out of the sleeves. Now that I can see his head, I can tell that it's a boy. "He thinks his jacket is a space suit."

Astra makes no effort to take off her solar jack. "I guess that's one of the perks of having a dead astronaut for a mom."

I can't believe Astra just said that, but Mr. Primm doesn't react, so I try not to react either. "I can take those," I say softly.

Mr. Primm strips off his solar jack and drapes it across my arms. "Thank you, kind sir," he says with a deep, back-breaking bow. "Your chivalry hath not gone unnoticed."

Mom's shoulders relax, and I grin despite myself. Mr. Primm may be a weirdo, but I like his kind of weird.

Astra rolls her eyes. "He's obsessed with the Middle Ages. He knows the routes, causes, and outcomes of all the numbered Crusades, and he claims he'd rather die of the bubonic plague than sun poisoning."

"What can I say?" Mr. Primm asks. "Chivalry is a lost art." He slugs Astra in the shoulder. "Your mother doesn't call me Don Quixote for nothing."

Mom's shoulders tense back up. Astra's eyes practically pop out of their sockets. Even Janus feels the strain—he stops gnawing on his bishop and looks up at Mr. Primm.

I can't see my face, but it feels like it's frozen. Not only is he talking about Dr. Primm, but he's actually *joking* about her—in the present tense.

"Not that I fight windmills or pursue shepherdesses," he goes on, completely oblivious to our distress. "But if I *did* fight windmills, I'd definitely take out their turbines. Jousting them is mostly useless, as Señor Cervantes showed."

I have no idea what Mr. Primm is talking about, but a snort still escapes my lips, punctuating the dead silence. I clap a hand over my mouth, but that just makes Mr. Primm smile.

"Dinner won't be ready for another few minutes," Mom replies as she retreats to the kitchen, "but you're welcome to come in and take a load off, if you'd like."

At the sound of the word *dinner*, Janus drops the spit-soaked bishop and makes a beeline for the kitchen. Mr. Primm saunters after him, leaving me alone with Astra.

"It's official," she mumbles. "My dad's in serious denial."

"She hasn't been gone for very long. He's probably still adjusting."

Astra shakes her head. "She's been dead for, like, three *months*, and yet Dad still seems to think she's gonna waltz through our front door."

I look down at my toes. "Maybe it's just his way of coping."

"Well, it's a bad way," Astra says as she rips off her solar jack and wads it up into a ball. She looks around the living room. "Where do you want our jackets?"

I look around the living room too. Except for the chess set—which Janus spit-polished—the furniture's covered with dust. It's pretty safe to say that we don't spend much time in here. If Mom is anything like me, it reminds her too much of Dad.

"We can dump them here," I say, chucking her dad's solar jack onto the couch. It's as good a place as any.

"Unless you think your little brother will try to maul them too?"

"Unlikely," Astra says as she tosses hers onto the pile. "He chewed through a space suit once and had gas for a whole week, so now he avoids synthetics."

I clap a hand over my mouth, but the laugh dies in my throat when I realize that Mom is doing the same thing with Mr. Primm. Her hand is on his arm, and whenever he says anything remotely funny, she tips her head back and cackles. They're so absorbed in their conversation that they haven't noticed Janus, who's been dipping his fingers into the carrot mousse.

Astra shoos him away, but the damage has already been done. When we finally sit down, I try to let Mom know that her dessert's been compromised. But after she waves me off for the third time, I decide to let it go.

Over her famous gnocchi soup, Mom drags out her where-were-you-on-the-day-the-world-started-ending story. Everyone had heard about the asteroid that was going to buzz Jupiter, so on the night of the flyby, hundreds of thousands of telescopes were aimed at the star-washed sky, hoping to catch the slightest glimpse. Mom was behind one of those telescopes—until she started throwing up for the sixth day in a row. While the rest of the world was hunched behind their telescopes, she was hunched over the toilet, emptying her steak-and-shrimp dinner into the bottom of the bowl. I was born exactly seven and a half months later.

Something sour floods my mouth, and it's not the fancy cheese that Mom reserves for this recipe. She didn't tell me that story until I stumbled home from school with snot cascading down my face after Benny Hargrave stole my lunch and told me I was nothing special. It belongs to *me* as much as it belongs to her. I can't believe she's sharing it with someone we barely know, with someone who *isn't* Dad.

When Mr. Primm compliments the cooking and Mom offers him a bite from her own spoon, I know I have to intervene. I try to catch Astra's attention, but she's too busy swirling her soup into a bowl-sized whirlpool. If I'm going to do something, I'm going to have to do it on my own.

First I take stock of my resources. The soup is Mom's pride and joy, the tastiest thing that she's come up with since the planet went to pot, but it's mostly colorless, so it won't make much of an impact. Plus it's still hot, and I don't want to hurt anyone. That leaves the loaf of lumpy bread, which we have almost every night, and the vat of carrot mousse, another of Mom's specialties. It's electric orange, and even more importantly, Janus' bodily fluids have already contaminated it.

Jackpot.

After making sure that Mom still isn't paying attention, I relocate the carrot mousse to the right of my elbow. Then I pretend to drop my spoon so I can give it a good whack. It tips end over end like a vat of bubbling tar, slopping onto the table before hitting the floor with a satisfying splat.

"Jameson!" Mom squeals. "What in the world are you doing?"

I look down at my toes. "Sorry," I say automatically, even though I'm not.

Mom inspects the mess, then presses her lips into a line. "Get a rag," she says, tipping her head toward the kitchen. "The program doesn't let us live here so we can destroy their carpet."

I don't bother to protest, just get up to get a rag. As soon as I leave the table, Mom gets another bite for Mr. Primm. I slam the rag drawer shut a little harder than I need to, but she doesn't seem to notice. By the time I get back to the table, I have so much angry energy rippling through my arms and legs that I don't have a problem scrubbing the carrot mousse out of the carpet. The stain comes out in seven swipes, but I stay on my hands and knees so I don't have to witness what's going on above my head.

I'm still scrubbing away when Astra pokes her head under the table. "Having fun down there?" she asks.

I take another swipe at the now-nonexistent stain. "Buckets," I say, scowling.

She cocks her head to the side. "What's your problem?" she demands.

My eyes flick toward Mom's black pumps, which are several inches closer to Mr. Primm's cracked leather loafers than they were when I got down here. "*Them*," I say with venom.

Astra blinks. "What's wrong with them?"

Do I really have to say it? "Don't you think they're . . . carrying on?"

Astra mulls that over. "And that bothers you," she says, somewhere between a question and a statement.

"Doesn't it bother *you*?" I hiss.

Instead of answering, Astra simply vanishes. Doesn't say a single word, just sits back up and disappears. A growl is building in my throat when she kicks me in the ribs. It surprises more than hurts me, and I buck despite myself. When my back connects with the table's underside, knocking our loaf of lumpy bread into the smear of carrot mousse, I know I've made a huge mistake.

"Jameson!" Mom says again. This time she doesn't sound surprised.

"Sorry!" I say again as I scramble to my feet. This time I actually mean it.

But Mom is coming unglued. Her neck turns red, then purple, and a dozen menacing emotions flash across her face. Finally the thunderstorm clears, but her voice is still low and lethal when she says, "Jameson, go to your room."

"It was an accident!" I say. I figure it's at least fifty-percent true.

"Accident or no," she says, "you've got to learn once and for all that actions always have reactions."

I open my mouth to argue, then snap it shut again. Astra's eyes are on her brother, who's stuffing gnocchi down his shirt, but she's shaking her head—at *me*.

And just like that, I get it. Astra bought me a ticket out of this horrible mess.

Cautiously I wad up the rag and chuck it into the recycler. I don't understand how or why she pulled it off, but I know an opportunity when I see one.

"Can I go with him?" Astra asks, turning her big brown eyes on Mom. She can be downright charming when she puts her mind to it.

Mom leans back in her seat. "Well, I guess—well, I don't know." She sneaks a peek at Mr. Primm. "What do you think, Carl?"

"It's your house," he says, shrugging.

Mom tucks her hair behind her ear. "Well, then it's probably all right." Still, she doesn't sound convinced.

"Thank you, Ms. O'Malley." Astra slurps down one last bite of soup as she hops out of her seat. "I promise I'll keep him out of trouble."

Somehow I doubt that.

I expect Mom to change her mind, but before she can get the words out, Mr. Primm asks for the bread. By the time she passes it, he's in the middle of a joke, and it's clear Astra and I have been thoroughly forgotten.

"That was brilliant," I whisper once we've cleared the dining room and are halfway down the hall.

Astra just waves me off.

"No, really, it was brilliant. I never would have thought to make an even *bigger* mess. . . ."

I trail off when I realize that she's no longer listening. She's frozen in my doorway, her gaze darting back and forth, and I see my room through her eyes. My bed is bolted to the wall to make the room look like a pod, and the walls are papered with star charts and various spaceship schematics. Highly detailed models of the *Amerigo Vespucci*, the *Millennium Falcon*, and the *Battlestar Galactica* are dangling from the ceiling on strands of hair-thin fishing line.

And that doesn't even count the JICC.

"What *is* that?" she asks without bothering to point.

"It's my JICC," I say proudly. "Well, the *J* stands for 'Jameson's,' so I probably should have said *the* JICC." I crinkle my nose. "But that still doesn't quite work, does it?"

"Who cares?" she asks. "What does it *do*?"

I slide into my chair with what I hope is a sly grin. "That's the most exciting part."

I could explain how the JICC works, but it will be easier to show her. I've been so preoccupied with today's dinner date that I haven't even turned it on in the past couple of days, so there's bound to be a message. I can feel it in my bones. My fingers tingle with anticipation as I jiggle the mouse, but when the monitor lights up, the message bar just sits there, blank.

Dad hasn't tried to contact me.

# 8

I JIGGLE THE MOUSE AGAIN, but the message bar doesn't respond.

Astra crinkles her nose. "What is it supposed to do exactly?"

"It's supposed to say, '*ONE NEW TRANSMISSION.*'" Even though it's only been four days, Dad always knows when I need him. And I really need him *now*, to impress the coolest girl I know. "My dad was supposed to send a message!"

"Your *dad?*" Astra replies. "I thought your dad was . . . gone."

"He isn't *gone* gone," I reply. But then, I shouldn't be surprised that she jumped to that conclusion. That's where her mom is, after all.

"Then where is he?" she demands, looking around the room like I'm hiding him under the bed or something.

"Where do you think he is? On Mars!"

Astra makes a face. "*My* dad was flirting with your mom while *your* dad is stuck on Mars?" She digs her fists into her eyes. "I wish I could un-see and un-hear everything from the last hour."

I nod sympathetically. "Dad has been on Mars for the last"—I glance at the calendar—"seven hundred and forty-one days. We built the JICC before he left so we could talk while he was gone."

Astra lowers her fists. "You guys *built* this?" she asks.

I puff up my chest. "You should see the antenna out back."

Astra looks over her shoulder as if she can see through walls, but if she can, she hasn't mentioned it. I keep typing in commands, every command I can think of, but none of them work. The JICC is as good as dead. I let out a primal howl and raise the mouse above my head.

Before I can let it fly, Astra jumps in front of the JICC. "Hey, don't shoot the messenger. You said you and your dad built this thing together, right?"

I lower the mouse. "That's right." Where is she going with this?

"Then don't destroy it while you're angry." Astra looks over the JICC, taking in the knobs and buttons. "Even if it doesn't work, it's still a part of you and him."

"It *works,*" I say, scowling.

"Whatever you say, chief." She's trying to sound tough, but when she checks left, then right, I can tell she's making sure that no one will overhear. "After my mom left, I started telling everyone that I was fixing up our boat so I could sail around the world, explore the underwater cities. It wasn't true, obviously, but I liked working on the motor and mapping out the quickest routes." She snorts under her breath. "I even had the neighbor convinced that my homemade scuba tank worked."

I knot my arms across my chest. "But the JICC *does* work," I say.

She doesn't bother to reply.

I huff impatiently. I can handle skepticism but not outright stupidity. "You see this box right here? It converts the satellite's signal into high-definition audio *and* video. And this contraption over here"—I tap a funny-looking gadget with a bunch of knobs and cylinders—"is a homemade superhet."

She leans closer to inspect it. "Does it have a crystal oscillator?"

I'm pleasantly surprised that she's familiar with the term. "You'd better believe it." I rack my scrambled brains for something else to show off. "Hey, do you want to check out our high-voltage relay? Mom says it looks like a doughnut."

"You have a high-voltage relay?"

"Of *course* we do," I say snootily. "How else did you expect us to boost a signal to Mars?"

Astra looks around the room. "Do you keep it in the closet?"

"What do you take me for, a moron?" I motion toward the backyard. "It's in the shed out back."

We're halfway down the hall when Mr. Primm's silhouette appears with a Janus-shaped solar jack draped over its shoulder.

"I think this little man had too much carrot mousse," he says, patting Janus on the back. The way that he pats his son's back, like he's the most precious of cargo, makes my mouth smile at the same time it makes my shoulders sag. "Are you ready to go, Astra?"

"I was going to show her our high-voltage relay," I reply, looking back and forth between them. "But you guys can come too."

"I'll have to pass," Mr. Primm says. "This monster needs to go to bed." He sends Astra a sideways glance. "But you can stay a little longer."

Astra doesn't answer right away, and my fingers start to tingle. If she doesn't go home, she'll be the first friend I've had over since I developed an adhesive compound with Elian Montoya and we accidentally-on-purpose glued his hands together.

But then Astra looks away and shoves her hands into her pockets. "Another time," she finally says.

I don't let myself deflate. "You could come over tomorrow." I hope I don't sound too anxious.

"Or anytime," Mom says as she comes up behind me. "You're always more than welcome."

Astra almost smiles as she puts her solar jack back on. "Thank you, Ms. O'Malley." Her gaze flicks in my direction. "I'll have to take you up on that sometime."

Mom walks them to the door and even manages to force the leftover carrot mousse on them, but I just stand there grinning. Astra wants to come back over. Maybe tonight wasn't a total waste.

* ⋆ *

I spend the rest of the night wondering if I should walk to school with Astra the next morning. I don't want her to think I didn't have an awesome time, but I also don't want her to think I immediately glom on to people and can't take a hint. Moonbeams move across my ceiling in slow, steady arcs, making it look like my model spaceships are hurtling through space. When the moonbeams finally surrender to the pale gray light of dawn, I manage to fall asleep, only to wake up an hour later—52 minutes after my alarm clock started beeping.

I leap out of bed, throw on the first set of clothes I find, and put my solar jack on inside out. While I'm trying to fix it, Mom tosses a piece of toast at me, which I don't manage to catch. Now I'll have to de-lint it before it will be edible. At least that occupies my hands, not to mention my brain waves, as I head out the door and make my way up Armstrong Street.

I've just polished off the final bite and am licking butter off my fingers when someone pokes me in the arm. I look over my shoulder, but strangely no one's there—until I turn back around. Astra's right in front of me, hands stuck on her hips.

"Holy cannoli!" I half say, half yelp, pressing a hand over my heart. I don't actually know what cannoli are, but since Mom won't talk about them, I assume they're dangerous. "What are you trying to do, put me into cardiac arrest?"

Astra only shrugs. "I was trying to *not* scare you."

"Well, you failed—epically," I say. I rub the back of my neck. "Why are you always so stealthy?"

She thinks about that. "Habit?"

Now that the shock has worn off, I realize *she* hunted *me* down. That's got to count for something.

"I want to come over," she blurts before we've even started moving. "To your house. After school."

I guess *that's* what it counts for. "Yeah, sure," I reply, wiping my sweaty hands on my pants.

Astra nods. "That's good. That's *great*."

I expect her to take off, but she falls into step beside me, making this the best and most terrifying walk to school *ever*. I keep trying to engage her in a dazzling conversation about the effects of solar wind or the program's latest hygiene memo, which limits handwashing to three seconds and teeth-brushing to eight, but every time I try to speak, she checks the time on her commie or bends down to tie her shoe.

As soon as we get to school, Astra nods and walks away. We spend the rest of the day basically ignoring one another (which is harder than it looks, since we're both in the same class). Whether that's a good thing or a bad thing, I honestly have no idea.

As soon as the bell rings, I half walk, half gallop home. Astra didn't say exactly when she would come over, so I have to be ready. According to Sol Santos, the most popular kid in the fifth grade, retro is the new modern, so I dig Settlers of Catan out of the back of my closet. Then I find my chemistry kit, since you really never know when you might need some mega putty. Last I head into the kitchen and rummage madly through the pantry, looking for something we can eat. I'm in up to my shoulders when I stumble across my tofu taco. Even though it slimes me, I can't bring myself to care. Astra is coming over. Astra's really coming over.

After recycling the mess and scrubbing the slime off my hands, I dive back into the pantry. The dehydrated carrot sticks say they're expired, but the protein cubes might work.

Mom pulls into the garage while I'm lining them up on the counter. "Please tell me you're not making dinner," she says as soon as she walks in.

"Astra's coming over," I explain.

"When?" Mom asks, perking up.

"It could be anytime," I say as I survey my handiwork. "I just thought it would be nice to have a few munchies on hand—"

I'm interrupted by three knocks. I send Mom a wide-eyed glance, then make a beeline for the living room and yank open the door. Astra's standing on the porch with her hands shoved in her pockets.

"You're here," I say breathlessly.

Astra steps into the house without waiting for an invitation. "Of course I am," she says, taking off her solar jack. Her hair is in one bun today, centered over her right ear.

I close the door behind her. "What do you want to do?" I ask. Then, without waiting for her answer, I rattle off some of our options: "I was thinking we could play some games or whip up a batch of mega putty, and I found these protein cubes in the back of the pantry—"

"Jameson," Mom interrupts with an enigmatic smile. "If you want Astra to decide, you're going to have to stop talking."

I open my mouth to answer, then snap it shut again. Hopefully they'll think the heat steadily rising in my cheeks is a leftover sunburn.

Astra clears her throat. "Actually," she says, "I was hoping we could use the JICC."

I crinkle my nose. "Use the JICC to *what?*" I ask.

"Send a message," Astra says, digging a toe into the carpet.

Mom presses her lips into a line. I know what she thinks of the JICC, so I'm astonished when she says, "I'll see if I can find some snacks."

"I already found some snacks!" I holler as Mom retreats into the kitchen.

"Some *better* snacks!" she hollers back.

I narrow my eyes, but Astra's already halfway to my room, and I can only follow one of them. The JICC doesn't like strangers, so I scurry after Astra, who's acting a little weird. There's so much spring in her step that she's practically skipping, and she hasn't stopped smiling since Mom mentioned better snacks. At least she has the decency to frown when she notices my scowl.

"Oh, come on," she says as she bumps me with her shoulder. "The JICC's your favorite, and you know it."

"It *is* my favorite," I reply. "But if Sol Santos were here, he'd want to play Settlers of Catan."

"First off," Astra says, "I don't know who Sol Santos is. And second, even if I did—or maybe *especially* if I did—I wouldn't give a flying fart."

I press a hand over my mouth, but a giggle still escapes. I've never heard someone put *flying* and *fart* together. It doesn't make a stitch of sense, but that just makes it funnier. Astra must think it's funny too, because she's trying not to grin.

I'm still trying to stop laughing—and Astra's trying not to start—when Mom appears with better snacks: a plate of warmed-up butter cookies and two extra-large glasses of reconstituted milk. I pounce on the butter cookies, but Astra doesn't even glance at them before she sits down at the JICC.

"Shanksh, Mom," I say around a mouthful of cookie.

"Yes, thank you, Ms. O'Malley," Astra adds distractedly.

"Call me Mina," Mom replies as she looks back and forth between us. "And it's the least that I can do." Her gaze lingers on the JICC as she backtracks toward the door, and for a second, maybe more, I think she's going to change her mind. But she just says, "No monkey business," then sweeps out of the room.

I wait for her footsteps to recede, then return my attention to Astra. She's typing in commands so fast that her fingers are a blur, but her commands are too complex. She must have started coding long before they made it part of the program's core curriculum.

"No, they're simpler than that," I tell her. "*UPLOAD, DOWNLOAD* . . . basic English."

Astra's fingers freeze. "All right, then, which is it?"

"Well, I guess that depends on what you want to do," I say.

Now her hands curl into claws. "What do you usually do?"

I tilt my head to the side. "The first thing I usually do is check to see if there's a message."

She scans the monitor. "Well, is there?"

I realize I haven't checked the JICC since I left for school this morning. I was too preoccupied with Astra's impending visit. My heart begins to pound—but the message bar is blank.

"No," I say tiredly. I sigh and drop my gaze.

Astra sneaks a peek at me. I sincerely hope my face is as blank as that dumb message bar.

"Now what do you do?" she asks.

"Now I usually sit around and wait for a new transmission to come in."

Astra nabs a butter cookie. "How long does that usually take?"

"On the days he sends a message?" I calculate the average in my head. "Somewhere around two or three minutes."

"Two or three minutes?" she replies. "So every time you turn on the JICC, your dad just happens to send a new transmission? What are the chances of *that*?"

"Well, not *every* time," I say. "But on the days he sends a message . . . yeah."

She folds her arms across her waist and munches on her butter cookie. "The transmission might not load until you turn on the JICC." She eyes it appraisingly. "I guess that could explain it."

I don't like the whiff of skepticism in her voice, but I don't have a better reason. "It *works*," is all I say.

She doesn't agree or disagree, just grabs another butter cookie. I grab another too, just to have something to do. Ten seconds pass, then twenty, then a full minute, then three. I'm on my fifth butter cookie when Astra finally asks, "How long are we gonna keep waiting?"

"As long as we have to!" I snap, then wish I could take it back. That was the opposite of friendly. "Sorry for yelling at you."

"Apology accepted," Astra says.

I glance at the monitor for what feels like the hundredth time. "It doesn't usually take this long."

Astra starts to say something, then changes her mind at the last second. Starts to say something again, then instantly thinks better of it. Finally she clears her throat and asks, "While we're waiting for a message from your dad, can we, uh, send one to my mom?"

I accidentally inhale my butter cookie. Astra pounds me on the back while my epiglottis fights to clear it. When she offers me a glass of milk, I chug the whole thing in one gulp, but not because I'm still choking. Now I'm just stalling for time.

Astra looks down at her hands, which are tangled in her lap. "I know everyone says my mom is dead. I know *I* say my mom is dead." She drags her hand under her nose. "But what if we're all wrong?"

What am I supposed to say to *that*? If Astra came to me for answers, she definitely came to the wrong place. I open and close my mouth like a malfunctioning recycler, but she doesn't try to fill the silence, just sits there watching, waiting, hoping.

Finally I force myself to say, "That would be a big thing to be wrong about."

"No," Astra replies, "it would be a big thing to be *right* about."

I can't argue with that. And I know how Astra feels. Sometimes it feels like Dad is just a transmission away, but other times it feels like he isn't even in the same solar system anymore. That's when I have to take deep breaths and tell myself that it's OK, that we'll see each other again, that we'll laugh at each other's dumb jokes and sit on the roof and watch the stars.

And Dad isn't even dead.

I lick the sugar off my lips, then quickly type in *UPLOAD* for her. As soon as Astra's face appears on the screen, she brushes the crumbs off her shirt. Her eyes are open wide, and she's not smirking or scowling. I like the way she looks when she's not trying to look fierce.

"It's recording," I murmur.

Astra nods once, resolutely, then sits up a little straighter. I lean back against my bed, careful not to make it creak, but her attention doesn't waver. I may as well be on Mars.

"Mom?" she peeps, then clears her throat. "I mean, Mom, it's me. Astra. I don't know if you can hear me or if you're even there, but if you are there, if you can hear me, I just wanted to tell you I'm sorry. I shouldn't have dumped my cereal all over you that morning. I was angry, so I did it, but it was stupid and plain mean. You and Dad taught me way better. I just wanted you to know." She half sniffles, half sobs. "Anyway, if you get this message, will you send me a message back? I'd really like to hear from you. OK, I guess I'd better go."

Silent tears spill down my cheeks, leaving salty tracks behind. A part of me wants to wipe them off, but another part just wants to leave them. Maybe she won't feel as bad if she sees that I've been crying too.

Astra sniffles one last time, then slowly rises to her feet. "Thank you for your help," she says as if we're in a business meeting. "If you hear from her, you'll let me know?"

I can't nod fast enough. "Of course."

"Well, then I should probably go." She looks around the room like she's just surfaced from a dream. "But maybe we could whip up a batch of mega putty next time?"

I grin. "That would be great."

"Until then," Astra replies, and with that, she slips away as silently as a shadow.

# 9

I'M STILL STARING AT THE DOOR Astra just disappeared through when Mom pokes her head into the room. "Did Astra go home?" she asks.

I nod tiredly.

She lingers in the doorway. "What did she want with the JICC?"

Astra's business is her own, but she didn't say I *couldn't* tell. And it's not like Mom's a gossip. She rarely talks to anyone.

I draw a careful breath. "To send a message to her mom."

Mom's eyes widen. "Jameson, her mom—you've seen the news—"

"I *know*, Mom," I interrupt. "But how could I say no?"

She considers that, then sighs. "Did she seem OK before she left?"

"As OK as she could seem." My voice is tiny when I add, "Mom, I don't know what to do."

She smiles softly. "Just be her friend, Jameson. And let her be yours."

That answer is so *right* that I can't believe it came out of Mom. I instantly feel closer to her. She's seemed so cold, so distant, ever since Dad left for Mars.

"Do you miss him?" I whisper. Judging by her startled look, I don't have to say who *he* is.

The question makes Mom flinch, but only for the briefest moment. "I miss him every day," she whispers, but instead of going on, she pulls the door closed behind her, leaving me to my own thoughts.

I let out a held-in breath. After last night's dinner date, I was starting to wonder. But I can't decide if her answer makes me feel better or worse.

I'm still puzzling it out when the monitor catches my eye. The message bar is blinking: *1 NEW TRANSMISSION.*

There's no way Dad could have gotten our message before he sent this one, but I type in *DOWNLOAD*, anyway.

"Hey, kid," Dad says weakly once the image resolves. It's another close-up on his face, so the bags under his eyes are clearly visible. "It's day seven forty-two, and I'm exhausted, just exhausted. A day up here may only be forty-five minutes longer, but you could have fooled me."

I squint at the monitor. Dad's shoulders are hunched, and the color of his skin reminds me of the inside of an apple after you cut it too soon. I wish I could ask him what was wrong and get an immediate answer. I wish I could have gone with him.

"I don't know how to say this gently, so I'm just gonna get it out—Haisheng has asked me and a small group of volunteers to scout the Valles Marineris. It's a long-term mission, so I'll be away from the colony for the next couple of months, maybe the next couple of years." When Dad rubs the back of his neck, I know what he's going to say before his mouth can form the words. "That means that I won't be around to send transmissions for a while."

It feels like someone landed a sucker punch to my stomach. Dad's captain is sending him to explore the second-longest canyon in the known solar system? This seems like the sort of news UNN would be all over, but I'm certain Hester Dibble hasn't even mentioned it.

I'm still trying to process this unexpected information when Dad buries his face in his hands. "What am I *doing?*" he mutters like he's talking to himself. He gets up to pace around the pod, then, finally, comes and sits back down. "All right, there is no long-term mission. Haisheng isn't sending me to scout the Valles Marineris."

The air evacuates my lungs. Dad just admitted that he *lied.* Has he lied to me before? I rack my brains for an example, but I keep coming up short. Of course, if he *has* lied—and never bothered to confess—there'd be no way for me to know.

Dad draws a bracing breath. "What I'm trying to say is that I may not be around for the next little while. I'm almost out of time—don't ask me why, I can't explain—so I don't know if I'll be able to send another message. But I want you to know that I love you, more than Olympus Mons is tall and the universe is wide." He looks down at his hands, which are clasped tightly together. "No matter where we go, I will always be your father, and you will always be my son."

The transmission ends before he says, "Mars to Jameson," and it's all that I can do not to fall out of my seat. What was *that supposed to be?* I force myself to type in *REPLAY*, but it makes even less sense the second time around. Why did Dad bother to drag Haisheng into his tall tale? Why didn't he just tell the truth?

# 10

AT FIRST I DON'T TELL ANYONE about Dad's latest transmission. If I don't talk about it, it can't turn out to be true. But after one day passes, then two, then three, then a full week, I know I have to tell *someone*, or I'm going to explode.

On Friday night, I weigh my options. I could talk to Dr. Ainge, but after waiting a whole week, I don't want to wait another hour, let alone two or three more days. Having a heart-to-heart with Mom would be the next logical choice, but she'd probably just brush me off. I know how she feels about the JICC.

And that's how I arrive at Astra.

I'm deciding how to tell her when a familiar-looking shadow peels away from the Primms' garage. It's towing a turquoise bike, so I assume it's Astra. She's probably heading to the roof. But before she pedals off, she sends me a sideways glance. The light in my room is off, so she can't possibly see me, but I crouch down instinctively. Then I remind myself that *Astra* is glancing at *me*.

We haven't exchanged more than ten words since she sent that message to her mom, but that glance seemed significant. It was probably a sign.

After poking my head out into the hall, I ease my door all the way shut and stuff my feet into my shoes. Mom's been giving me my space—it's almost like she's sensed something going on—but I don't want to press my luck. Besides, sneaking out will be way more exciting.

The main characters in Dad's old spy novels sneak out all the time, but the first thing I learn is that it's not as easy it sounds. Once I wrench the window open, I have to pop the screen out, and then there's the tricky matter of getting my legs through the opening. I've barely climbed onto the ledge before I fall off the other side.

At least I land in the dirt instead of back in my room. That would have been *really* embarrassing.

The wind is surprisingly cold, cutting through my thin clothes like an ice pick. Even though the sun has long since set, I wish I had my solar jack. It would be warmer than this shirt. But I'm *not* climbing through that window more than once tonight, so I decide to keep going. I could take the hoverboard, but that would only make it worse, and Wheelock Park isn't *that* big. Besides, it's not like I don't know exactly where Astra is headed.

Except I don't find Astra anywhere near the roof. She's waiting for me at the end of Armstrong Street, twirling her pedals impatiently.

"Took you long enough," she says.

I stick out my chin. "Well, excuse me for having less experience than you."

The words fly out of my mouth before I can reel them back. I expect Astra to scowl, maybe fire off a glib one-liner, but she just thumps me on the shoulder, hard.

"I've been waiting for you to sprout a backbone." She motions toward her bike. "Can I offer you a ride?"

"Oh, I don't . . . pedal," I say. I can't quite bring myself to tell her that I don't know how to.

Astra shakes her head. "I wasn't offering to let you pedal." She motions toward the handlebars. "I was offering to let you *ride*."

It takes me a few seconds to put the pieces together. Then, reluctantly, I clamber up onto the bike. I've never tried to ride on someone's handlebars before, so I have to make it up. I start by straddling the wheel, grabbing hold of the crossbar, and trying to climb onto the pegs.

"Not that way," Astra says, pushing me back onto the ground. "You have to face out, not in."

Swallowing, I turn around and fumble blindly for the crossbar. But even once I've found it, I don't know what to do next. Boost myself onto the handlebars? Defy the laws of physics?

"Hang on tight!" Astra says, yanking me up by my armpits and setting me on the crossbar.

I don't have a chance to scream before she's pedaling full-speed, so I do the next best thing—I take my feet off the pegs and try to get us to slow down.

"Stop wiggling!" she shouts. "Are you *trying* to crash us?"

"I don't know," I mutter back. "Are you trying to get Branislav's attention?"

She leans forward. "What was that?"

"I said, are you *trying* to get Branislav's attention?" I try to turn around, but that's easier thought than done. "He's the guard—"

"Don't turn around!"

Her warning comes too late—I've already thrown us off balance—and then we're tripping, flipping, flying, a jumble of wheels and limbs. I wasn't paying attention to our route, but when we happen to fall into the Francos' gravel pit, I know exactly where we are.

"I crashed us," I croak as I struggle to sit up.

Astra rolls onto her knees. "No, *I* crashed us," she replies. "Do you know how many yards have a gravel pit by the sidewalk?"

"Just this one," I reply, spitting grit out of my mouth.

Astra's teeth flash. "*Exactly.*"

I inspect my knees, which took the brunt of the impact. Except for the second-degree road rash, they look like they'll be all right. I sneak a peek at Astra, but she seems more concerned about her bike than she is about herself. Eventually she picks it up, then motions for me to follow her.

After stashing our mode of transportation under the Brandts' skeletal hedge, we let ourselves out through the gate and dash across Main Street. When we reach the ladder, Astra laces her fingers and points her chin up at the sky. I know without having to ask that she's offering to give me a boost.

My knees have finally stopped throbbing, but it still takes me ten minutes to make my way up the ladder. As soon as I reach the top, I flop onto the ledge like a dying anglerfish and suck deep breaths through my mouth. Astra is nowhere near as winded. She pulls herself over the ledge as sleekly as an alley cat, landing in a wary crouch.

It's only once we've settled into our desk chairs and propped our feet up on the crates that she says, "You need to work on your upper-body strength."

I half laugh, half snort. "I need to work on my *full*-body strength."

Astra scrounges up a bag of stale banana chips. "You're good at leading with your weaknesses."

I knot my arms across my chest. "You sound like Dr. Ainge."

She shrugs. "So do you."

I can't decide if that's an accusation or a simple statement of fact, so I let the subject drop—and realize I'm no longer shivering. You'd think it would be colder up here, more exposed to the elements, but the desk chair I'm sitting in is radiating heat. I guess that's just what happens when you're mostly made of metal and exposed to the broiling sun for ten to twelve hours every day.

Thinking about the sun makes my thoughts circle back to Mars, and thinking about Mars makes my thoughts circle back to Dad, and thinking about Dad makes my thoughts circle back to Astra and the mom I still haven't heard from. The JICC hasn't had any new transmissions in a whole week.

I'm trying to decide how to break the news to her when Astra finally says, "I know what you're trying to say, so you can man up and just say it."

I raise my eyebrows. "You do?" I'm not sure *I* know what I was trying to say.

Astra nods knowingly. "If you'd heard from my mom, you would have told me right away." She pulls out a banana chip, gives it a thorough inspection, and flicks it over the ledge.

I know she must have more to say, so I fight the urge to interrupt.

"The truth is, I already knew—that she's gone, I mean." Astra looks down at her hands. "I guess you make it easier to look on the bright side of things."

That could be the nicest thing she's ever said to anyone.

She gives another poor banana chip a thorough inspection, then pops it into her mouth. "You must have heard from your dad, though." She offers me the bag. "So what did he have to say?"

I hold my hands up to refuse it. Or to refuse her question. It's a toss-up at this point.

Astra sets the bag aside. "Jameson," she says. Somehow she must sense that there's something I'm not saying. "What did he have to say?"

"It was weird," I finally say, replaying the message in my head. "He said Haisheng, his captain, had a new mission for him, one that could take him away from the colony for *years*. But, like, two seconds later, he admitted he was lying, and *then* he mumbled something about being out of time."

Astra's eyes narrow. "Has he lied to you before?"

"Not that I know of," I reply.

"So now you think he's hiding something." It doesn't come out as a question. "Now you think something is wrong."

I can't bring myself to nod, but she seems to understand.

"But you haven't gotten any news? There's been no official visit?"

"What do you mean, 'official visit'?"

Astra sniffs. "You know, the glitz, the glam, the presentation of the flags. They tell you they're *very* sorry, but not as sorry as you are."

I can no longer meet her gaze. "Is that how it happened for you?"

The question makes her flinch, but she doesn't try to dodge it. "Janus had been crying and, like, digging at his ears, so we'd just gotten back from a trip to the doctor's. Two decked-out Marines were waiting on our porch. Mom's boss at the university was with them." She looks at me, then looks away. "They asked if they could come in, but Dad said, 'No, just tell me here.' So they told us. On our porch. Not that we were shocked by that point. When two Marines and a department head show up out of the blue, you know it's probably not good news."

That actually makes me feel better. "Well, they haven't sent Marines or a department head," I say. "But you think they would have if he—"

"Yeah." She must not want me to go on. "So it must be something else. Maybe something with the JICC."

"I already told you, the JICC works."

"Maybe it did," Astra replies. "But maybe it doesn't anymore."

# 11

THE NEXT AFTERNOON finds us holed up in my room, clenching screwdrivers we plundered from Dad's old tool chest. There's a wild gleam in Astra's eyes, but my stomach is tied in Gordian knots.

"Wait," I say, blinking, as Astra raises her screwdriver. It reminds me of a bloody dagger; the only thing that's missing is the blood. "Let's think this through for a minute."

"What's to think through?" Astra asks. "The JICC was alive, and now it's dead."

I lick my salty lips, tightening my grip on my screwdriver. "But what if we . . . break it?"

"It's already broken!" she replies. "Honestly, Jameson, what are you waiting for?"

What *am* I waiting for? I honestly can't say. I just know that I'm not ready to tear my heart and soul apart. But I can't admit that either.

I glance anxiously around the room, looking for something, *anything*, to put off Astra's eagerness. I find it in an unexpected place: *Long-Range Communication Systems for Beginners and Non-Beginners.*

"Maybe we should check this out," I say as I lunge to grab the book. It's even heavier than I remember, so it tumbles off my nightstand and hits the ground with a thud.

She cranes her neck to read the title. "*Long-Range Communication Systems for Beginners and Non-Beginners?* Where the heck did you get *that?*"

I climb onto my bed. "From Dr. Ainge, of course."

Astra doesn't challenge that, but she doesn't put her screwdriver down either. Desperately I flip it open to the table of contents—and nearly slam it shut again. I've always been a fan of textbooks, but even I have never seen so many subsections within subsections.

Astra makes a face. "Please tell me you don't intend to read that whole thing before we start."

I pretend to be unfazed. "It seems like we should at least *skim* it."

"You skim it," she replies, raising her screwdriver once more. "I'll get to work on the dissection."

A part of me is tempted to take her screwdriver and fart on it, but we're not seven anymore. I start skimming instead, hoping to find something we can use before she tears the JICC apart. The first couple of chapters are just a rambling introduction—Dad says that only stupid people have to convince you that they're smart—so I get through those pretty quickly. The third chapter is little more than a dictionary, but the fourth chapter looks promising.

"Listen to this," I say without looking up at her. "'A disruption-tolerant network, also known as a delay-tolerant network or a DTN for short, is an ambitious grand-scale network designed to cope with the pitfalls—'"

"Sum it up," Astra cuts in.

I scan the paragraph again. "Basically I think it's saying Earth-based protocols won't work for interplanetary networks. When you type in a URL, your IP address pings the server of the website you're trying to go to and requests an access point. If it doesn't get an answer in the first one-point-five seconds, it gives up and drops the ping because it was set up to *assume* the network would be reliable. But interplanetary networks are way less reliable—because of the planets' alignment and a million other things—which means those networks need to be more disruption-tolerant."

"How do they do that?" she asks.

"With a specialized transmitter capable of *storing* data instead of just transmitting it. In a full-fledged DTN, if a transmitter gets a ping it can't immediately process, it hangs on to the request—and the information that came with it—until it can transmit again."

"Fantastic," she replies. "But we don't *have* a DTN."

"We can build one. With a SAFe card."

Astra shakes her head. "Never heard of it," she says.

"It stands for 'store-and-forward' card." I happen to glance down at the floor, which is now cluttered with spare parts. "Oh my gosh, what have you done?"

"I told you I was gonna get to work." She wipes her forehead on her sleeve. "I figured we could leave the actual computer alone, since you clearly didn't build it, but I've broken down the router, the translator, and the superhet." She gestures toward each pile of copper and silicon in turn. "Don't worry, I logged everything, so it shouldn't be too hard to put the pieces back together."

I push the book aside and get down on the floor with her. As I sift through the pieces of carefully shaped metal, I remember doing the same thing when my fingers were much smaller and the pieces seemed much bigger. The workbench came up to my chin then, so I couldn't always see what Dad was doing, but I remember he once said I'd be better at this than he was someday.

I wish that someday were today.

While I've been strolling—or slogging—up and down Memory Lane, Astra has been reading. "According to this bit," she says, tapping the bottom of the page, "we shouldn't even need the superhet."

"*What?*" I half ask, half gasp. The superhet converts the signal to a more stable frequency so the rest of the receiver can interpret it more easily. There's no way we can ditch it.

Astra turns the book around to face me. "Doesn't it look like a SAFe card is just a beefed-up Wi-Fi card?"

I jerk the book out of her hands—she can't possibly be right—but it turns out that she is. A SAFe card is just a part that turns a boring, old computer into a DTN transmitter that can store and forward chunks of data.

She tilts her head to the side. "We'll have to reconstruct your router and reconnect some of the transfers. Keeping your computer wired in to your gargantuan antenna should make the signal less susceptible to the delays they talked about. And I guess we'll have to open up your computer after all." She seizes a loose piece of paper and copies down the diagram. "But before we do anything else, we should get our hands on one of these."

"I bet the commissary has one—and I bet my mom can drive us."

We leap to our feet in unison and race each other to the door. Astra gets there first, but when she gets to the end of the hall, she stops to let me catch up. I lead the way into the kitchen, where we find Mom dicing peaches.

"Hey, Mom," I say casually. If she knows we're working on the JICC, we might be done before we start, so I have to proceed with caution. "What have you been up to lately?"

"Oh, you know, just making dinner." She scratches her forehead with the back of her wrist. "What have *you* been up to lately?"

I feel the heat crawl up my neck, but luckily Mom's still looking down, so she doesn't seem to notice. "Oh, you know, just doing . . . stuff." When Astra nudges me, I add, "Actually we've been tinkering with this wicked science project, but we ran into a snag, so we were wondering if you could take us over to the commissary."

"A science project?" Mom replies.

My mind immediately goes blank, but Astra doesn't miss a beat.

"It's for school," she says breezily. In fact, she sounds so convincing that *I* almost believe her. "Mr. Rix asked us to design and build a rain gauge that can withstand a Midwestern monsoon."

Mr. Rix *did* ask us to design and build a rain gauge that can withstand a Midwestern monsoon, but we wrapped that up last week. I start to correct her, but before my mouth can form the words, Astra digs her heel into my instep. I growl despite myself, and Mom finally looks up.

"Are you OK?" she asks.

"I'm peachy," I reply, fighting the urge to rub my foot.

Mom eyes me for another moment, then, finally, sets down her knife. "I guess I can spare an hour." As she grabs her solar jack, she asks Astra over her shoulder, "Your dad's not working tonight, is he?"

Astra's smile is serene. "Oh, I'm pretty sure he is."

Mom doesn't reply, just tips her head in acknowledgment, but I'm pretty sure one corner of her mouth curls up. I force myself not to gag as I stuff my arms into my solar jack and fall into step behind them. Mom can flirt with Mr. Primm until the astronauts come home—or at least until Dad does—if it means Astra and I can get our hands on this part.

# 12

AS SOON AS WE STEP THROUGH the commissary's giant door, Mom checks the time on her commie. "You have exactly sixteen minutes."

This doesn't seem like enough time to walk up and down an aisle, let alone find a SAFe card, but Astra doesn't seem to mind.

"No problem," she replies as she takes hold of my wrist and tugs me the other way. "We'll meet you back here in twenty."

"Make it fifteen!" Mom calls after us.

Astra's only reply is to drag me deeper into the commissary. It feels like we're just wandering, turning random corners, but I get the impression that she knows where she's going.

"Where are we going?" I ask, just to prove my theory right.

"To find Tallulah," she replies.

I don't know who or what a Tallulah is, but since Astra seems to know, I don't press her for details. She guides us through the labyrinth as expertly as a pathfinder, and it's not long before we're standing under a floating *HARDWARE* sign.

"Tallulah!" Astra says.

When a spiky-haired woman wielding a clipboard whirls around, I learn what a Tallulah is. Her scowl could probably send the Great Waste into a deep freeze, but as soon as she spots Astra, it morphs into a grin.

"Astra!" she replies. They do some weird handshake thing that involves lots of slapping and snapping. "Haven't seen you in a while. I heard you were on house arrest."

"The reports of my grounding have been greatly exaggerated."

Astra doesn't introduce me, and Tallulah doesn't ask. I can't decide if she knows who I am or she simply doesn't care.

I like her already.

Tallulah folds her arms across her waist and hugs the clipboard to her chest. "So what brings you to these parts?" Then she jabs me with her elbow and points her chin at the sign. "Get it? 'These parts'?"

It takes me a few seconds to remember where we are. "Oh right. Hardware. Good one." I force myself to laugh.

"We're looking for a SAFe card," Astra says as she pulls out her diagram and passes it over to Tallulah. "It's for a . . . science project."

Tallulah whistles, long and low. "You're looking for a SAFe card?" she replies. "Those are *way* above my pay grade." She gives Astra back her diagram. "You'll have to check with Harold."

Astra makes a face. "You're really sending me to *Harold*?"

Tallulah checks her clipboard but not very thoroughly. "I'm sure it's a special, so if you want the SAFe card, you're gonna have to go through him."

"Who's Harold?" I ask.

"The most insufferable human being in the solar system," Astra says.

Tallulah pats her back. "Good luck."

I have no idea what to expect based on these answers, but as it turns out, Harold is the head of Special Items, the only department in the commissary kept under techno-lock and tag. He has bright purple hair and a quills-and-inkwell tattoo, which he rubs absently as he peruses a textbook on quantum mechanics.

"Good afternoon, Ms. Primm," he says once he finally looks up. He's positioned himself so he's perfectly framed in the techno-locked door behind him. "How may I be of assistance?"

Astra rolls her eyes. "We both know you hate me as much as I hate you, so feel free to cut the crap."

He sets the manual down with a thump. "All right, then, Primm. What do you want?"

She pulls out her diagram again, then, after checking both ways, carefully unfolds it and slides it across the counter. "Just give us one of these, and we'll get out of your hair."

Harold barely glances at it before he flicks it aside. "That's impossible," he says.

Astra grits her teeth. "Nothing's *impossible*," she says. "You just don't want to give it to us because you're a jerk and a coward."

Harold's nostrils shrivel into slits. "On the contrary," he says, "I don't want to give it to you because *you're* a ten-year-old."

"I'm eleven," Astra snaps as she cracks her knuckles threateningly.

I decide now might be a good time to insert myself between them. "I have a bunch of base credits stored up, so I can pay for the SAFe card—"

"It's not a matter of *paying.*" He weaves his arms across his chest. "It's a matter of allocating resources to the worthiest causes. Do you really think we'd give a *SAFe card* to a couple of children?"

Astra starts to answer, but I raise a hand to stop her. Wrecking balls only destroy.

"I get that you have to make the tough calls," I reply, sliding my backpack off my shoulders and pulling out Dr. Ainge's book. When Harold doesn't tase us, I set it on the counter and flip it to page 107. "But this isn't just your run-of-the-mill project. We're tackling hard science."

Harold cocks an eyebrow and slides the book closer. I wait expectantly, but after studying the plans and flipping through the next few pages, he just slides it back to me.

"It's a worthy project," he says, "but I can't disperse a special without prior approval."

I feel my chest deflate, but Astra won't admit defeat.

"Then let's get Mr. Ishii down here." She leans across the counter, seizes Harold's hidden radio, and brings it to her lips. "Can we get Mr. Ishii to come down to Special Items?"

Astra's voice echoes through the store. No more than a few seconds later, a distant door closes. I glance over my shoulder just in time to see a stocky man descending the metal staircase that runs up a nearby wall. He must have come out of the office that looms above the commissary.

We're still awaiting Mr. Ishii when Mom appears out of the woodwork. "I thought that was you," she says, looking Astra up and down. "What do you two think you're doing?"

I pat the book weakly. "Still looking for that part."

"But this bozo over here"—Astra flicks a thumb at Harold—"keeps getting in our way."

Harold's nostrils flare, but before he can get a word in edgewise, Mr. Ishii bustles up. Mr. Primm's not far behind.

"What do you think you're doing, Harold?" Mr. Ishii demands. "Customers are *not* allowed to use your private radio!"

Harold's nostrils flare again, but this time, it's Mr. Primm who won't let him get a word in edgewise.

"So that *was* you," he cuts in as he grabs Astra by the shoulders. "Are you OK? Why are you here?"

"I brought them," Mom admits. "They said they needed a part."

"A *SAFe card*," Harold says, "which we don't hand out to just anyone."

I stick out my chin. "We're definitely *someone*," I reply. Astra must be rubbing off on me.

Harold sticks his nose in the air. "You two may think you're special, but you're not special enough."

I open my mouth to answer, then snap it shut again. I didn't mean to imply that we deserved special treatment.

Astra sets her sights on Mr. Ishii. "Come on, Mr. Ishii. You can override this clown."

Mr. Primm squeezes Astra's shoulder hard enough to make her wince, but before Harold can object, Mr. Ishii cuts him off.

"I'm sorry, Ms. Primm," he replies, "but we have to reserve these items for unique or pressing cases." He eyes the *SPECIAL ITEMS* sign hanging over Harold's head. "That's kind of the whole point."

"But this case *is* unique." Astra points her chin at me. "Without a SAFe card, Jameson won't be able to talk to his dad!"

Four pairs of eyes zoom in on me. I melt under their scrutiny and lower my gaze. But when I finally muster the courage to raise it again, they aren't looking at me. They're looking at Mom.

She snakes an arm around my shoulders. "I'm sorry we wasted your time," she mumbles to Mr. Ishii. Then she tries to steer me toward the door.

I shake off her arm. "That's it?" I reply. "You're just going to apologize? To *them*?"

"It's their policy," she murmurs. But it doesn't sound like she means it.

My vision narrows to a single point, and I can't see, can barely breathe. The universe took Dad away, and now Mom's turning on me too. I back away from her, from Special Items, from the world. By the time I realize what's happening, I'm halfway to the door.

"Jameson!" Mom calls after me, but I don't even slow down. At this point, I would rather take my chances with the sun.

* ⋆ *

There's nowhere to go but home. It will be an awful walk, but I don't want to wait for Mom. At least I can track my progress based on the number of fuel tanks that I pass.

After adjusting my solar jack, I shove my hands into my pockets and start walking. I've only made it past one fuel tank when the Light-Year catches up. Mom must have left Astra behind. Even though I'm barely moving, Mom manages to keep pace with me. At least she doesn't try to talk. She must sense how far she's pushed me.

I don't know how far we've gone—maybe a mile, maybe less—when I start to rethink my plan. I'm not breathing so much as wheezing, and my legs feel like spaghetti. I guess righteous indignation can only carry you so far.

"Jameson," Mom finally says after I don't quite get my foot down and have to lurch to catch myself. "Will you please get in the car?"

I press my lips into a line and take another halting step.

We half roll, half plod along the abandoned stretch of road that will take us back to Wheelock Park. Sweat pours down my forehead, but my eyebrows catch most of it before it drips into my eyes. Still, I can barely see. The sunlight is so bright that it's reflecting off the asphalt.

"Get in the car," Mom says. It's a command, not a suggestion. When I do nothing, she adds, *"Please."*

I'm not sure if it's her tone or my general lack of fitness, but my resolve starts to weaken. I can feel the cold air pouring through the Light-Year's open window and puddling around my feet. It dissipates into nothing almost as soon as it hits the blacktop, but if I were to climb in, Mom would roll that window up and crank the air conditioning. That's one of the perks of living on a dying planet—you can stop obsessing about your carbon footprint.

Mom must sense my hesitation, because she doubles down. "I wish I'd understood what this SAFe card thing was for, and I'm sorry that I didn't. But you can't put yourself in danger." Her breath catches in her throat. "If something were to happen to you, if you left me here by myself . . ."

I miss my step again, but not because of my spaghetti legs. When Dad left for Mars, he didn't just abandon *me*. For some reason, that thought has never crossed my mind before.

I must have stopped walking at some point—I don't know exactly when—so the Light-Year also stopped. Without saying a word, I grab hold of the latch and crawl into the passenger seat. Now that they're not holding me up, my legs decide to spasm, but Mom's shoulders still sag as I pull the door closed behind me.

"*Thank you,*" is all she says.

Whether she's thanking me for finally getting in the car or for not leaving her behind, I honestly can't tell. Maybe it's one and the same.

# 13

WHEN I LEAVE FOR SCHOOL on Monday, I find Astra waiting for me at the bottom of my driveway. Her solar jack's visor is locked firmly into place, but I can still see the mischief gleaming in her curious brown eyes.

"Should I be afraid?" I ask.

Astra doesn't take my bait. "I know how we can get a SAFe card."

I can't help but shiver as I glance over my shoulder. Mom's not lurking on the porch, so there's no way she overheard, but I steer Astra down the street before she raises her voice.

"All right, what's your plan?" I ask.

Astra's eyes light up like a pair of rocket boosters. "We get ourselves to the commissary and find a place to hide until it closes. *Then* we use my dad's tag to deactivate the techno-lock behind stupid Harold's desk."

I can't help but gulp. Using her dad's tag will be risky. The program issues tags for security reasons, and everyone on the base has one. You're supposed to keep your tag in your pocket at all times, but since mine won't be encoded with more than my name and birth date until I turn eighteen, I've tucked it into my sock drawer. Mr. Primm's a grown-up, though. If he finds *his* tag is missing, he'll probably sound the alarm.

"How do you know his tag will work?"

"Because Mr. Ishii likes him. He programmed my dad's tag with *every* deactivation code on my dad's second day there."

"Well . . . where will we hide?" I ask.

Astra smiles smugly. "Leave the hiding place to me."

"That's all well and good," I say, "but you're forgetting one small thing."

She doesn't stop smiling. "Only one?"

I don't bother to respond to that. "How are we supposed to get to the commissary in the first place?"

"That's the microscopic flaw in my otherwise grand plan. But I'm sure you'll think of something."

"Why do *I* have to think of it?"

"Because," she says, beaming brightly, "you're the one who needs the part. And I've planned everything else."

I guess I can't argue with that.

Astra and I lapse into silence as we trudge up Armstrong Street. I count sidewalk squares to keep myself from going crazy. Counting always helps me think.

I've come up with and discarded at least a dozen ideas— the best involved my hoverboard, but I'm not sure it has the range—when Astra claps and says, "I've got it! We can hijack your mom's car."

"You can't be serious," I say.

"Well, we can't steal my dad's car. It would stick out like a sore thumb."

"We're *not* stealing my mom's Light-Year. For one thing, the program could track it. For another, we can't drive."

"Suit yourself," Astra replies, folding her arms. "But don't say I didn't help."

"There has to be another way. We must know someone else who drives."

It's not until we get to school that I spot the solution to our problem: Evelyn Segundo. She's not a grown-up yet, so I doubt she'll ask too many questions. She and Braxton Fitzwilliam are exchanging witty banter, so I sidle up to her and wait for them to finish chatting.

"Jameson!" she says once Braxton finally wanders off. Her gaze flickers to Astra, then swiftly flickers back to me. "What have you been up to lately?"

"Oh, not much," I lie, then clear my throat and drop my gaze. "Actually we were wondering if you could give us a ride. To the commissary. Tomorrow."

Evelyn's nose crinkles. "What could you possibly need there?"

Sometimes I forget that Evelyn hates the commissary. She grew up in Miami in a sixty-story high-rise. When the ocean started gobbling up huge chunks of Florida, her family got stuck in their 27th-floor apartment. They lived on bottled water and canned beans until the Coast Guard rescued them more than three months later. Now they live on next to nothing so that natural disasters will never catch them off guard again.

"A blender," Astra says while I'm still fumbling for an answer.

Evelyn cocks an eyebrow. "A blender?" she replies.

Astra doesn't even flinch. "It's for a secret science project."

Evelyn eyes Astra, then sends me a sideways glance. I put on my most honest face and pray that I don't get struck down.

"Why can't your mom drive you?" she asks.

"Dentist appointment!" I blurt awkwardly.

Astra doesn't miss a beat. "But my dad can drive us home."

Evelyn eyes her one more time, then, finally, sighs and says, "All right. Meet me in the commons tomorrow afternoon at three." She turns to go, then turns right back. "But you can't borrow my credits! Even though I have a ton!"

Astra makes a face. "We wouldn't dream of it, Your Dorkiness," she says with a deep bow.

I fight the urge to smack my forehead. Someone needs to teach that girl how to relate to other human beings.

# 14

I REVIEW THE PLAN a hundred times over the next 24 hours, poking and prodding it for problems, but as much as it pains me to admit it, Astra's plan seems pretty sound. By the time that I wake up, I'm feeling good about the plan, convinced we've thought of everything.

Except a Midwestern monsoon.

Evelyn meets us in the commons at three o'clock on the dot, then silently leads us to the door closest to the rear parking lot. But that's as far as we make it.

We huddle inside that back door, watching the rain descend in waves. The pools of muck it leaves behind would reflect the slate-gray sky if they weren't clogged with the debris that the wind is kicking up—and the parking lot is partly sheltered.

According to Mr. Rix, this part of Minnesota didn't used to get monsoons. Even though Earth is heating up, it still has as much water as ever. The water cycle's just messed up, so now it opens the valve less predictably than it used to. In other words, when it rains, it usually floods.

Evelyn cranes her neck to catch a glimpse of her Light-Year. "Are you sure you want to go? Won't your parents be concerned?"

Mom thinks I'm doing homework in Ms. Pearson's open lab, and Mr. Primm thinks Astra's trying out for the fifth-grade gravball team. By the time they realize we're not where we said we would be, we should already be well hidden somewhere in the commissary.

I shake my head and say, "We're sure."

Evelyn half nods, half shrugs. "Well, then let's shake and bake." She glances at Astra, who's glaring daggers at the doorknob. "Coming, sunshine?"

Astra sends her a dark look, then shoves the back door open and stalks out into the rain.

I don't have a chance to blink before a wall of wind and water hits me, instantly soaking my pants and snatching the breath from my lungs. It's like showering in a wind tunnel.

And I'm still standing inside.

Not to be outdone by Astra, Evelyn zips up her solar jack and plunges into the storm, leaving me no choice but to stumble after them. I try to keep an eye on Evelyn, but every time I raise my chin, a shotgun blast's worth of rain hits me between the eyes. When my outstretched arms run into Evelyn's Light-Year, it's nothing short of a miracle.

I find the passenger door more by feel than sight. The wind tries to tear it away when I pop it open, but somehow I yank it closed before the hinges give out. After scrubbing out my eyes, I glance over at Evelyn, who's climbed into the driver's seat. She's sneaking peeks at Astra.

"What is she waiting for?" she asks. "A personal invite?"

Astra has stopped next to the car, head tipped back toward the clouds, arms spread out like wings. There's something kind of cool about taking on the elements, but Evelyn must not agree, because she honks her horn. Astra ignores her for another couple of seconds before she climbs into the back.

Evelyn eyes her in the rearview, but she manages to hold her tongue. "Buckle up," she says, waving her program-issued tag in front of the car's techno-lock. "It's going to be a splashy ride."

As it turns out, "splashy" doesn't even begin to describe it. By the time we reach the end of Main Street, we've already driven through three elbow-high puddles and accidentally clipped a curb.

"Keep going?" Evelyn asks.

"Keep going," Astra says.

Evelyn cocks an eyebrow at me, but I don't know what to say, much less what to do, so I say and do nothing. With a heavy sigh, Evelyn turns onto the road leading to the commissary.

"So about this science project," she finally says once several miles have slid past us. "Is it for Mr. Rix's class?"

"Yep," Astra replies at the same time I say, "Not really."

Evelyn clucks her tongue. "If you're going to collude, it helps to get your story straight."

I feel the heat crawl up my neck, but she doesn't press us for details, just mumbles something to herself about her night-vision goggles and digs around in the glovebox. Her eyes aren't on the road when Astra sticks both legs straight out and presses herself into her seat.

"Sandbar, SANDBAR, Evelyn!"

Evelyn looks up just in time to whip the steering wheel around and mash the brake into the floor. I dig my nails into the armrest, too terrified to speak, but there's no slowing our momentum. The Light-Year spins around six times before it slides into a streetlight, and we whiplash to a stop.

The rain pummels the roof as we just sit there, barely breathing. The rain is so relentless I can't pick out single raindrops, so instead of counting those, I imagine that we're floating, drifting silently through space. I focus on that feeling until my pulse decelerates and my lungs resume breathing.

Evelyn snaps into action, pawing at her seat belt until it finally comes undone. "Is everyone OK?"

I nod woozily.

Astra ignores Evelyn's question. "Now what?" she demands.

Evelyn pulls out her commie. "Now we call for help."

Astra seizes the commie. "But if we call for help, they'll take us to the infirmary."

Evelyn snatches it back. "We've just been in an accident." She fiddles with her commie with one hand and jabs the Light-Year's power button with the other. It just clicks and clicks. "I think a trip to the infirmary would be a good idea."

Astra shakes her head. "*I think a trip to the infirmary would only slow us down.*"

I can't decide who I agree with, so instead of taking sides, I lean back against the headrest. The rain sounds less soothing now; its rat-tat-tat-tatting makes me think of a machine gun. And the seconds just keep ticking by, each one lowering our chances of getting our hands on a SAFe card.

By the time the medics roll up in their hulking medi-tanks, the rain has started to die down, but the wind is still howling like a wounded animal. The medics check us out, but except for the small bump on the back of Astra's head, they seem to think that we're OK. Unfortunately the same thing can't be said for Evelyn's Light-Year.

"We'll have to come back for it later," the head medic says grimly. "Where would you like us to drop you?"

"Wheelock Park," Evelyn says at the same time Astra replies, "The commissary would be great."

The head medic cocks an eyebrow, and six pairs of eyes zoom in on me. I want to crawl into the car and let someone else decide, but we're out here for the JICC, and the JICC is on my shoulders.

"You can take her home," I say, pointing my chin at Evelyn, "but Astra and I need to get to the commissary."

# 15

AT FIRST THE HEAD MEDIC doesn't want to take us anywhere but home, but when Astra explains that her dad works at the commissary—without mentioning, of course, that he doesn't know we're coming—he agrees to drop us off. A retrofitted medi-tank is way more solid than a Light-Year, so it doesn't even wobble as it braves the gale-force winds.

When we pull into the parking lot, I don't want to get out, not with the wind still screaming madly, but Astra has other ideas. After saluting the head medic, she drags me out into the rain.

As soon as the medi-tank chugs off, Astra checks the time. It's 7:29, 31 minutes until closing. Good thing we left so early, or we might not have made it.

"Come on," Astra says, ignoring the autobaton standing guard next to the door. "There's something cool I want to show you."

I'd rather find a place to hide until everyone clears out, but Astra has this pesky habit of always getting what she wants. I trail along behind her as she struts up the nearest aisle like she owns the whole dang place. When people stop to stare, either because they recognize her or because she's oozing confidence, I lower my gaze and put more distance between us. Astra just ignores them, keeping her sights set straight ahead.

Shame makes me hunch my shoulders. Dad wouldn't have avoided them. He would have asked where they were from and said something to make them laugh. He would have turned them into friends.

Astra spreads her arms open wide. "Don't you love this place?" she asks as we turn down aisle 19.

I want to say, *Love is kind of a strong word*, but that doesn't sound daring enough, so I settle for, "Yeah, sure."

If Astra notices the tiny wobble in my voice, she's kind enough to let it go. But then she shoves me in the shoulder. Before I can catch myself, I fall into the shelving unit. It isn't long before I'm drowning in a sea of strange white fluff.

Astra dives in next to me. "*This*," she says emphatically as she tucks her hands behind her head, "is the best spot in the whole store."

I struggle to breathe. "What are these things?" I demand.

She motions toward the label overhead, which reads *SYNTHORGANIC DOWN PILLOWS*.

"What is synthorganic down?" I ask.

"Who knows?" Astra replies, burrowing down a little deeper. "But honestly, who cares?"

Even though I feel uncomfortable making myself at home, I follow Astra's lead and try to let myself relax. Whatever this stuff is, it's soft, squishy, and slightly suffocating. Or maybe more than just slightly. It's closing around my face, and I can't seem to catch my breath.

As I scrabble for the surface, I realize I'm drowning not in pillows but in guilt. We're buried in a mountain of who even knows what, and every single atom has been paid for by the program. How can I steal from them when they've fed and clothed me my whole life? But how can I *not* if I want to talk to Dad again?

I must be hyperventilating, because Astra surfaces. "You're not wimping out on me, are you?"

I can't wimp out. I *won't*. Not if Dad is on the line. "Of course not," I reply. I hope I sound more confident than I feel deep down inside.

Astra seems to understand. "Come on," she says again, less excitedly this time. "I know the perfect hiding place."

Without another word, Astra leads us down the aisle and around two or three corners. Within a matter of minutes, I'm thoroughly, hopelessly lost, but somehow Astra seems to know where we are and where we're headed. Mr. Primm must have brought her to Take Your Daughter to Work Day.

We've just reached aisle 86, *CAMPING AND OUTDOOR EQUIPMENT*, when a disembodied voice announces, "The commissary will be closing in exactly fifteen minutes. Please proceed to checkout. The commissary will be closing in exactly fifteen minutes. Please proceed to checkout."

Proceeding to checkout is the last thing we plan to do, but the other person in this aisle, an older man with wiry nose hairs, startles at the sound of the voice, then mutters something at the ceiling. His clothes look like they haven't been laundered in several weeks, but the armband on his solar jack, which features a halo stitched above a helicopter, is still clearly visible. He used to be a Chopper Dropper.

When the oceans started rising and officials realized they weren't going to retreat, there were hordes of people stranded on both sides of the country. The Coast Guard sprang into action and organized teams of rescuers to save as many as they could. They swooped over flooded cities in their orange helicopters, plucking people from apartments—or wherever they might be—and ferrying them to higher ground. They spent months and years on the front lines of a battle they didn't really understand, exposing themselves to the worst nature had to offer. By the time everyone realized the sun was killing them, the effects were irreversible. Now the program feeds and shelters them as a way of saying thank you.

I creep closer to the man so I don't have to shout at him. "Excuse me, sir?" I ask.

Astra looks up from the camping stove she's been fiddling with, then quickly looks away again when she spots the Chopper Dropper. Her reaction makes me wince. The Chopper Droppers scare people because they're not right in the head—overexposure to the sun will do that—but I would have thought that she'd be different. That she would understand.

"Excuse me, sir?" I ask again. I hope he hasn't lost his hearing. "Is there something we can help you with?"

This time I can tell he hears me, because he startles again. He sends us a sideways glance, but we must not look too threatening, because he doesn't retreat.

"I can't seem to figure out which of these doohickeys I want." He looks back and forth between two identical lamps. "Can you tell which one's solar-powered?"

I creep even closer, then, when he doesn't object, close the distance between us. I didn't think the program made any other kind of lamp, and sure enough, they're both solar-powered.

I'm trying to decide how to break the news to him without making him feel bad when Astra peers over my shoulder, then snorts loudly in my ear. "They're identical, old man—"

"What she *means*," I interrupt, sending her a dirty look, "is that both should work just fine." I take the one out of his left hand and return it to the shelf, then nod toward the one in his right. "I think you should get that one."

"This one," he says dreamily, like I've just proven that Einstein-Rosen bridges are for real. "Yes, I think I'll get this one. You have my sincerest thanks, Mr. . . . ?"

"Jameson," I finish, hesitating only slightly. Mom says I shouldn't give my name to random people on the street, but certainly this Chopper Dropper doesn't mean me any harm. "And you're welcome, Mr. . . . ?"

The Chopper Dropper doesn't answer. His watery eyes narrow instead. "Jameson," he says, tilting his head to the side. "Don't I know you from somewhere?"

I shouldn't have given him my name. Strangers do strange things with your name. "I don't think so. Probably not."

The Chopper Dropper nods. "OK." His gaze drifts over to Astra. "Nice to see you, Astra Primm."

And with that, he wanders off, presumably to get his lamp. I can't help but frown as I watch him disappear—the fact that he recognized Astra means he must still watch the news, so he can't be too far gone—but Astra taps her foot and breathes through her mouth obnoxiously. She sounds like an air filter in desperate need of replacement.

"*Finally*," she says once the Chopper Dropper turns the corner.

"That was a Chopper Dropper. After everything he's done, you could show him some respect."

"*You* show him some respect." Astra grabs hold of the shelf that the camping stoves are on. "*I'll* be over here, stealing the SAFe card for *your* JICC."

I force myself not to react. I should have guessed how she'd respond to seeing a Chopper Dropper. They must remind her of her mom.

"What are you doing?" I reply.

"See those tents up there?" she asks, nodding toward the highest shelf. "We're hiding in the biggest one."

I gape at the tents, then at the sky-high shelving unit. "What *is* it with you and heights?"

She considers that, then shrugs. "No one ever looks up."

Sighing, I grab hold of the lowest shelf and pull myself onto it. The shelves are barely shorter than we are, but if we use the boxes as step stools, we *might* be able to climb them. By the time we pull ourselves onto the third or fourth shelf, I've fallen into a smooth rhythm of stepping, grabbing, and pulling.

I just can't let myself look down.

We've just reached the top when the disembodied voice says, "The commissary is now closed." I can almost hear it smiling when it adds, "Good night."

The lights turn off in unison, and a small gasp escapes my lips. If I didn't know better, I'd think a black hole had swallowed us. But no sooner have the lights gone out than dozens of flashlights flicker on.

Astra sidles up to me. "Closing protocol," she whispers. I can't see her face, but I can see the winking flashlights spreading out like a virus. "The program monitors each building's energy output, so as soon as the store closes, they turn off the overheads. But they still have to sweep the store."

I assume she knows about the protocol because her dad works here, but my heart still skips a beat. "What if they find us?" I reply.

"Oh, that's easy," Astra says. "They'll call your mom and my dad and throw us into the brig. Oh, and we won't get the SAFe card. That will be the worst."

My hearts stays in my throat as my eyes track the flashlights' progress. It doesn't take me long to spot the pattern—one flashlight for every four aisles, up and back and up and back—but some flashlights move faster than others. The one that will check our aisle is still two aisles away.

Easygoing sounds—the murmur of small talk interspersed with random chuckles—drift up from the ground, but they just make me more nervous. By the time the flashlight reaches the end of our aisle, I've nearly forgotten how to breathe.

At the bottom of our shelving unit, the flashlight flickers to a halt. My breath catches in my throat, but Astra claps a hand over my mouth before I can give us away. The flashlight's beam sweeps left, then right, then, finally, sails over our heads. I cringe away from it, but the boxes block our silhouettes.

Astra tucks her hands behind her head and leans back against a pole, but I don't let myself relax until the flashlights have converged on the commissary's door. They click off one by one, and lightning bolts illuminate the store as the door opens and shuts. The flashlight wielders disappear into the night. When the door slides closed for the last time, I finally let myself relax.

For a long time, we just sit there breathing as we listen to the shelving units creak. Now that I'm not focused on flashlights or finding a place to hide, I can hear the storm again. It sounds like hundreds of aliens are tap-dancing on the roof.

I swallow, hard. "Now what?"

"Now we climb down," Astra says.

Climbing down isn't as hard as climbing up, but that's mostly because I lose my grip on the last shelf and tumble the rest of the way. I hit the ground with a dull thud, but it's the way the shelving unit rattles that has me more concerned.

I wait for something to happen—an alarm to sound or a manager to bust us—but I'm still just sitting there waiting when Astra lands beside me in a crouch.

"Graceful," she says matter-of-factly.

"Yeah, well, we can't all be half cat."

Even in the dark, I can make out Astra's smirk. "Meow," she says sarcastically.

Astra may be half cat, but even she can't see in the dark. I'm about to ask how she plans to navigate the darkened aisles when she pulls a penlight out of her solar jack's pocket. She points it at her face and flicks it on, turning her familiar features into a mask of bumps and ridges, then aims it down the aisle and sets off determinedly.

I scowl at her retreating back, but I have no choice but to follow. We need that SAFe card desperately, and I couldn't find my way even if the lights were *on*.

"Special Items, twelve o'clock," Astra says a while later.

At the edge of her penlight's trail, I spy Harold's spotless counter. We exchange an eager look, then race each other down the aisle.

"I've always wanted to do this," Astra says, scrambling onto the counter. After doing a quick dance that involves scraping off her shoes, she lands smoothly on the other side and shines the penlight in my face. "Coming?"

Planting both hands on the counter, I boost myself onto its surface and swing my legs over the side—though, to be completely honest, I somehow over-rotate and end up falling off the edge. At least we both end up on Harold's side of the counter.

"And now," Astra says grandly, pulling her dad's tag from her pocket, "for the moment we've been waiting for."

I can't help but hold my breath as she waves Mr. Primm's tag in front of the techno-lock. A part of me expects it to glow red, since I *know* they have a bunch of autobatons lying around, waiting to capture would-be thieves, so when the techno-lock just clicks, that part of me feels almost cheated.

"They should have better security," I grumble as Astra shoves open the door.

"Or maybe they should just be way less stingy with their SAFe cards."

She waves her penlight from side to side, revealing a long corridor lined with plain gray doors. I tense when I spot a humanoid shadow at the end, but the autobaton doesn't react, just sits there sulking in the corner. It must need a system upgrade.

While I've been preparing to do battle with a broken autobaton, Astra's been scoping out the doors. "I've never been back here," she admits, "so we might have to try them all."

I draw a bracing breath, then swiftly turn the first handle. The door slides open easily, emitting a warm breeze that smells faintly of vinegar. Curious, I reach for the light switch.

"Don't turn the lights on!" Astra hisses, shining the penlight in my face. "The program monitors energy output, remember? They'll know that someone's here."

I raise a hand to shield my eyes. "Then I'm going to need your fancy light."

Grudgingly she hands it over, and I shine it around. It only takes me a few seconds to see why it smells like vinegar—there's nothing in here but pickles.

"It isn't in this one," I say as I let the door swing shut.

Astra reclaims her penlight and throws open the next door, but when I sneak a peek over her shoulder, the only thing I see is a blank room.

"Or in this one," she replies.

I crinkle my nose as the door closes on its own. The next two rooms are just as bad: bottled water and wool sweaters, though why they keep wool sweaters under techno-lock and tag, I honestly have no idea. But when we open the fifth door, the metallic tang of circuitry is unmistakable.

"Spread out," Astra says, setting the penlight on a workbench in the middle of the room. The walls are lined with narrow shelves, giving us lots of spots to check. "The SAFe card has to be here somewhere."

The penlight's glow is weak at best, but my fingers know their way around a workbench even better than my eyes do. I touch a ribbed rectangle that must be a motherboard and a pinwheel-shaped cylinder that's clearly a case fan. My pulse pounds in my ears—with each piece I eliminate, I know I'm getting closer—but I still haven't found anything that feels like a SAFe card when something scrapes out in the hall.

"Did you hear that?" I whisper as I glance over my shoulder.

"Hear *what*?" Astra replies. She doesn't look up from her shelf. "You're just freaking yourself out."

Swallowing, I set my sights on the next shelf to the left. The penlight is pointed this way, so if I squint, I can make out the familiar outline of a Wi-Fi card. Anticipation makes me rush to slide it out of the way, and sure enough, two matching SAFe cards are sitting on the shelf beside it.

I grab one of the SAFe cards. "Astra, I think I found—"

I don't have a chance to finish before a dozen laser sights hit me squarely in the chest and a dozen tinny voices shout, "Get your hands where we can see them!"

# 16

THE AUTOBATONS don't waste any time, just pick us up by our collars and drag us out into the hall. I don't resist, but Astra doesn't seem to know how *not* to. When her flailing fist connects with one of the autobatons' joints, it finally sets her down. She makes a mad dash for the door, but she only makes it a few steps before one of the others grabs her and tucks her under its arm.

Bathed in artificial light, the corridor looks ordinary. The walls are a plain gray, and what I thought was an autobaton lurking at the end of the hall turns out to be a potted plant. While the autobatons ferry us back up the hall, I stare down at my feet to avoid their blank expressions. I almost wish that they would yell.

When we reach the door, an autobaton pushes it open, and the ones behind it shove us out into the store. The lights out here are bright, way brighter than they were before, and I blink instinctively. They must have been desperate to find us.

I expect the autobatons to stick us in an unmarked Light-Year that will take us to the brig, but when they veer off toward the staircase bolted to the nearest wall, I fear that it will be much worse. Visions of interrogation rooms start parading through my brain, but when the lead autobaton knocks abruptly on the door, it's not opened by an executioner but by a pinch-faced Mr. Primm.

"Jameson!" he says. It sounds like he's surprised to see me. He pulls out his commie and presses it against his ear. "Mina? I found Jameson, and he looks fine, just fine."

I wince despite myself. "She's here?"

Mr. Primm covers the mouthpiece. "She's at your place watching Janus." Then he uncovers the mouthpiece. "Yes, Mina, I'm still here. And yes, he's OK."

Mom's sob carries through his commie, and I wince despite myself. I never thought that Mom would worry. I never thought she'd even *know*.

Mr. Primm looks over my shoulder. Suddenly his face un-pinches. "*Astra*," he half says, half breathes.

Astra doesn't meet his eyes, though I can't say I blame her. He looks slightly nauseous now, but just a few seconds ago, he looked mad enough to spit.

"Put her *down*," Mr. Primm says, practically shaking with rage. I can't tell who he's more upset at, Astra or the autobaton that's treating her like a fence post.

The autobaton puts Astra down, but not before clipping her heels on one of the metal railing's crossbars. Mr. Primm pushes the autobatons up against the wall as he forces his way past them. The staircase isn't wide enough, but he's determined to reach Astra. Probably to make sure she's OK.

"*Astra*," he says again, once he's finally standing above her. He takes her by the shoulders and peers into her nut-brown eyes. "You need to know how much I love you."

Whatever I thought he would say, that definitely wasn't it. I expect her to pull away, but she burrows in instead, snaking her arms around his waist and smashing her face into his chest.

I feel the heat crawl up my neck and force myself to look away. It feels like I'm intruding on something private, something sacred.

I'm still staring at my toes when an unfamiliar voice from somewhere in the office says, "Autobatons, you are dismissed."

One by one, the metal guards clatter back down the staircase. I don't realize that one of them has been clamping my left wrist until it finally lets go and I can feel my hand again.

"Mr. O'Malley?" the voice calls. This time I recognize it as Mr. Ishii's voice. "Would you be so kind as to step into my office so the Primms may do the same?"

I don't have a chance to answer before Mr. Primm drags Astra up the stairs and through the door. The railing digs into my back as I lean out of their way, and then I have no choice but to follow them inside.

"Shut the door," Mr. Ishii says once I've slipped into his office. He steeples gnarled fingers in front of surprisingly thin lips, then draws a cleansing breath and slowly lets it out again. "My apologies for the rough handling just now. I'm afraid the autobatons can be a little overeager."

Astra barks out a laugh. "Try malicious," she replies.

I press my lips into a line. Does she have to provoke *everyone?*

Luckily Mr. Ishii lets it go. "They're less costly than Marines—less prone to mischief-making too—and since trouble *usually* stays away from what we're doing here, I've found that they're mostly acceptable." He motions toward the plastic chairs that line the nearest wall. "Would you like to sit down?"

I nearly stumble in my haste to reach one of the plastic chairs. I've learned that when adults ask if you want to sit down, they're not really offering so much as ordering. Mr. Primm follows my lead, but Astra stays right where she is, arms knotted across her waist.

Mr. Ishii doesn't seem to care. "I see from the autobatons' feeds that you were found in Special Items." He looks back and forth between us. "Were you looking for a SAFe card?"

"We were," I say agreeably at the same time Astra says, "We're not saying a word without our lawyers in the room."

It's all that I can do not to chuck a pencil at her.

"And how exactly did you breach our closing protocol?" he asks.

Astra ignores this question. "How exactly did you know we were here in the first place?"

Mr. Ishii clears his throat. "When Carl called to tell me that his tag had gone astray—and that his daughter had too—I put two and two together." He leans forward in his seat. "Now how about you answer mine? I reviewed the vids myself. There were no disturbances."

I keep my mouth screwed shut—Astra must have some crazy answer she's been saving for this moment—but this time she says, "We hid. What else would we have done?"

Mr. Primm half grunts, half growls, but Mr. Ishii is unmoved.

"Where?" Mr. Ishii asks, tilting his head to the side.

She sticks both hands on her hips. "Do you really think we'd tell you?"

"ASTRA!" Mr. Primm replies.

She has the decency to flinch, but she still doesn't answer.

"In a tent," I race to say.

Astra scowls in my direction, though I can't quite decide if it's aimed at Mr. Primm or me. I wince and look away. It's not like I *meant* to betray her. I just don't know how to ignore authority figures.

Mr. Ishii nods. "In a tent," he says thoughtfully as he strokes his stubbly chin. "I guess we'll have to install some kind of anti-camping sensor."

Even I can tell his joke is only borderline funny, but I force myself to laugh. It comes out more like a wheeze. Mr. Primm winces and digs something out of his ear.

Mr. Ishii sets his sights on Astra. "Is it fair to say at least that you took your father's tag?"

"I didn't *take* it," Astra says. When Mr. Ishii cocks an eyebrow, she blushes and lowers her gaze. "I only borrowed it."

"*How?*" Mr. Primm replies, leaning forward in his seat. "It was in my pocket this morning. I swear I never took it out."

"You didn't take it out. *I* did."

Mr. Primm's nose crinkles. "When?"

"Remember when I 'tripped'"—Astra makes air quotes with her fingers—"on our way out to the car and you literally lunged to catch me?"

"You took advantage of my kindness to *pickpocket* me?" he asks.

"Jameson needed your tag."

I send her a wide-eyed glance. When Astra said we could use her dad's tag on the techno-lock, I assumed that meant that she would come up with a story and he'd let us borrow it. But before I have a chance to explain this to Mr. Primm, Mr. Ishii clears his throat.

"I assume you're aware of article two, subsection D of the program's manifesto, which prohibits the possession of another person's tag? And of article nineteen, which bans the misappropriation of the program's scarce resources?" When Astra doesn't flinch, he adds, "Both are third-level infractions."

I roll my tongue around my mouth. It's as dry as the Great Waste. They threw Evelyn's mom into the brig for no less than sixty days after she convinced the driver of her food delivery truck to give her an advance on her barleymeal allotment. They said it was a breach of the program's manifesto.

"We didn't mean to violate those articles," I say.

"And yet, Mr. O'Malley, that is precisely what you did."

"But that wasn't what we meant. It isn't like we're terrorists." When Mr. Ishii only blinks, I lick my lips and race to add, "I mean, we're not your average terrorists." I am *not* saying this right. "I mean, we're just average kids."

Astra kicks me in the shins, and I have to squelch the yelp that tries to clamber up my throat. I couldn't have handled that much worse. Mr. Ishii watches this exchange with a carefully neutral expression. I try to tell myself that the flicker in his eyes is a twinkle, not a spark.

"Given that you're minors and that this is your first offense—and that I like Carl so much—I've decided to release you on your own recognizance."

It's all that I can do not to fall down at his feet. I really thought that we were done for.

"But please be advised that I *won't* be so lenient should I find you here again in the future." He looks back and forth between us. "Do I make myself clear?"

"*Extremely* clear," I say.

"And do you agree, Ms. Primm?"

Astra doesn't bother to look up. "I guess."

I can't tell if she's upset because we got ourselves caught or because we didn't get the SAFe card. Either way, I think we're mostly getting off scot-free.

Mr. Ishii scoots his chair back. It squeals like the newborn piglets that Mom sometimes has to feed, since the slaughter yards are right next to the shadehouses. "Well, then I think we're finished here." He offers Mr. Primm his hand. "Thank you for letting me know that your tag had disappeared."

Mr. Primm shakes it eagerly. "My pleasure, Mr. Ishii. It was the least that I could do." He keeps shaking the man's hand. "If you need anything else, I'd be happy to assist. . . ."

Mr. Ishii waves that offer away. "Just take these whippersnappers home." He calmly extricates his hand. "They look ready to collapse."

I *feel* ready to collapse. Thankfully Mr. Primm agrees. He bows to Mr. Ishii, then sends us an icy glare and flicks a thumb over his shoulder. We trail along behind him—out the door, then down the stairs, then through the automatic door—like a pair of ugly ducklings.

I hug my arms around myself as I survey the parking lot, which now resembles a small lake. At least Mr. Ishii got an official transport for us. It's another retrofitted tank, this one with a passenger bay. The driver, a tall woman with red lips and slicked-back hair, extends her hand to Mr. Primm.

"Back to Wheelock Park?" she asks.

Mr. Primm half nods, half sighs.

She waves us into the transport. "Then let's go, let's go, let's go!"

We make a break for the transport. Though it's only a few yards away, I'm completely waterlogged by the time we reach the curb. I scamper up the ladder more by feel than sight, since the rain is blinding me. I only know I've reached the top once I run out of rungs to grab.

As we collapse into our seats, the transport rumbles to life. The rain hammering the roof echoes so loudly down here that I can feel it in my teeth, but I try to focus on Astra. She comes to sit by me instead of over by her dad, but she still hasn't said one word. Her anger is a wall I don't know how to penetrate, but I know I have to try.

"I'm sorry I dragged you into this," I say as quietly as I can.

She drags a hand under her nose. "I'm pretty sure *I* was the one who dragged *you* into this," she says.

"But you did it for my dad."

"And for you," Astra replies.

A spark of hope flares in my chest. Even though we're in huge trouble, it feels nice to have a friend.

# 17

BY THE TIME WE CHUG TO A STOP between my house and the Primms', the wind's almost died down, and it's just raining, not pouring. Still, Mr. Primm tries to protect us as we thank the transport's driver and gallop over to my porch. The front door tries to stick—it doesn't like Midwestern monsoons any more than the rest of us— but I'm in a worse mood than it is. We spill into the house, bringing several quarts of wet sludge with us.

It only takes me a few seconds to survey the living room. Mom's lava lamp is burning in the middle of the coffee table, turning the living room into an underwater cave of sorts. Dad's chess pieces have been strewn from one end of the carpet to the other, and Janus is sprawled out next to them, snoring lightly through his mouth. Mom is snoozing on the couch, but when the door slams shut behind us, she jerks instantly awake.

"Jameson?" she slurs like she's still mostly asleep. Then her eyes settle on me, and her pupils dilate to the size of silver dollars. She leaps up off the couch, crosses the room in two great strides, and pulls me into a hug. "Do you have any idea how *furious* I am right now?"

Mr. Primm shifts uncomfortably. "Thanks for watching Janus, Mina." He scoops his son up easily.

Mom doesn't reply. I can feel her trembling through our hug.

"I guess we'll just be going." He sends Astra a long look. "Say goodbye to Jameson."

She waves halfheartedly. "See you, Jameson," she says, but it sounds more like, *Hope you don't die.* She sends Mom a sideways glance as she slithers out of the house. Mr. Primm follows.

Mom doesn't wait for the door to close before she lets herself erupt. "What were you thinking?" she demands. "Honestly, what were you *thinking?*"

My throat seizes up, and I don't know if I can speak. "It doesn't work," I croak as tears puddle in my eyes. "How can I talk to Dad if the JICC isn't working?"

"That's no excuse," Mom says as she paces back and forth. Her eyes are on her toes, and her voice sounds far away. "We *never* should have kept that thing. I never should have gone along with it."

Now the tears are more than puddling. I knew Mom didn't like the JICC—in fact, she's *never* liked the JICC— but the venom in her voice is enough to make me flinch.

"But the JICC is Dad," I peep.

"That machine is *not* your father. It's not even a stand-in."

Before I have a chance to ask her what she means by that, Mom vacates the living room, fleeing down the darkened hall. I've never seen her this upset, not even when I cracked a rib trying to fix the satellite. I know she's mad at me—and I know that I deserve it—but what if she decides to take her rage out on the JICC?

I gallop down the hall, my pulse pounding in my ears. Dad keeps a hammer in his nightstand; Mom knows that as well as I do. If I can make it to the hammer before she gets to the JICC, I can keep the situation from devolving into something she and I will both regret.

I press my lips into a line and make the turn into her room, but Mom's not going for the hammer. She's curled up in a ball in the middle of the floor, sobbing uncontrollably.

I can take Mom's rage but not her unhappiness. A part of me wants to creep away and wait for her tears to dry up, but it's not like she's a stranger I can just choose to ignore.

"I'm sorry," I whisper as I kneel down next to her. But then I realize that she probably couldn't hear me, so I gulp and try again: "I'm sorry I lied to you."

Mom sits up suddenly. Her cheeks are wet with tears, and her eyes are webbed with thin red veins. I expect her to yell more, maybe send me to my room, but she doesn't say a word, just wraps her arms around my shoulders and presses her face into my neck.

I freeze despite myself. Her head is heavier than it looks, and now her sobs are threatening to tip both of us over. For a second, maybe less, I wish that Mr. Primm were here so she could cry on *his* shoulder. Then I remember how Mom used to pat my back when I was scared, so I pat hers tentatively.

I'm not sure how long it takes, but she finally—*finally*— stops. Dragging a hand under her nose, she sniffs and straightens up again. Her cheeks are still shiny with tears, but she's not crying anymore.

"No, Jameson, *I'm* sorry."

I crinkle my nose. "For what?"

Instead of answering, Mom presses a damp kiss to my cheek. I wait for some kind of explanation, *any* kind of explanation, but she just ruffles my hair and says, "It's time to go to bed."

* ⋆ *

I'm not sure what to expect when I wake up the next morning, but if you don't count Mom's red eyes, it's like last night never happened. I get dressed while she eats breakfast, and then she brushes her teeth while I make some powdered eggs. I'm still working up the nerve to ask what she's sorry about when she says she'll call ahead and warn Dr. Ainge.

*Warn her about* what? I want to ask, but the words snag in my throat. I don't usually see Dr. Ainge on Wednesdays. They must have decided that I need an intervention.

Sighing, I shrug on my solar jack and shuffle out the door. Though the Midwestern monsoon blew itself out overnight, random heaps of junk—tumbleweeds, roof tiles, even the spare solar panel—now decorate the neighborhood. And that doesn't count the sand. It's strewn across the road and piled up against the windward sides of Wheelock Park's houses. Crews will clean up the debris, but they won't bother with the sand. There's simply too much of it.

As I plod down Armstrong Street, my solar jack crinkles like static. I count my steps to keep from wondering where Astra is and what she's doing. When I finally reach the school—656 steps later—I find myself surrounded by a clump of gawking kids.

I can't see past, so I have to wait for the group to scatter to see what they're looking at. But as soon as they disperse, I wish that I could call them back. A horde of UNN news vans has taken over the drop-off, and at the center of the chaos is—you guessed it—Davis Darwin.

"Jameson!" he shouts, waving one arm over his head. He's the magnet; I'm the pole. "Jameson O'Malley, over here!"

I try to squeeze between a pair of hand-holding twelfth graders, but they both turn at the last second, effectively hemming me in. Before I have a chance to find another escape route, Davis Darwin has me cornered.

"What a coincidence," he says as if we just bumped into each other.

"It's seven minutes before school on a Wednesday morning," I say dryly. "Where else would I be?"

Davis Darwin ignores me. "Would you like to make a statement on the break-in at the commissary? Word on the street is that it was perpetrated by some kids."

It's a darn good thing I'm channeling my inner Astra, because my inner Jameson would have peed his pants by now.

"You don't happen to know who the culprits are, do you?"

I force myself not to react. He doesn't know I was involved. If he did, he would have parked his news van in the middle of my driveway.

"I don't know anything," I lie, making a beeline for the school. The words taste sour on my tongue, but I'm too scared to take them back.

Davis Darwin is undaunted. "How's your girlfriend?" he hollers, cupping a hand around his mouth. The question zings over my shoulder like a misfired bullet. "That good-for-nothing minx still owes me a new microphone!"

It's all that I can do not to fall flat on my face. How he connected me to Astra, I honestly have no idea. Not that I bother to respond. I tell myself it's just because I can't be late for my appointment.

As soon as I set foot in the office, the room goes completely still. Mr. Flores jams the pause button on the copy machine, and Ms. Cook's mouth snaps shut so swiftly I can hear her molars click. I guess Mom talked to them too.

"Have a seat!" Mr. Flores says, too brightly. "Dr. Ainge will be able to see you in another few minutes—"

He doesn't have a chance to finish before Dr. Ainge's door creaks open. I crane my neck to see who's there and lock eyes with Astra, who instantly freezes.

"Hey," I say with what I hope is the right amount of nonchalance.

She drops her gaze and mumbles, "Hey." She doesn't say anything else, just makes a beeline for the door.

*Astra, wait!* I want to yell, but she's already disappeared.

I'm still just standing there gaping when Mr. Flores clears his throat. I force myself to take a step, then another, then another. Last night I was thrilled we didn't get thrown into the brig, but now I can't help but wonder if that might have been better.

Dr. Ainge is spraying down her plants when I poke my head into the room. The program forces her to use reconditioned water, so the water in her spray bottle is an unsettling brown. "Come in, Jameson," she says.

I slide one foot through the door, then, when nothing awful happens, drag the other one behind it. Her office looks the same, but for some reason, I feel different.

"You look tired," she says simply.

I start to yawn despite myself, then force myself to close my mouth. This must be some kind of test. "I didn't get much sleep last night."

Dr. Ainge tilts her head to the side. "Oh?"

I know she wants me to go on, but I'm not in the mood to blather.

Instead of pumping me for details, she nods toward my usual plastic chair. "Well, then you'd better sit down."

I lower myself into the club chair, just to keep her on her toes.

She sets her spray bottle down. "What would you like to talk about?"

I hate it when she plays the open-ended-question card, but I probably should have seen it coming. "Mom told you about last night?"

She nods carefully. "She did."

"Well, then you already know." Suddenly my thoughts flit to the horde of UNN news vans outside. "She didn't tell *Davis Darwin*, did she?"

"I doubt it," she replies. "There are sensors everywhere, and UNN keeps as many eyes on them as the government does. They probably knew about the breach as soon as Mr. Ishii did. He managed to hold the jackals off until you made your escape. I wouldn't have known you were involved if your mother hadn't called."

I let myself relax a little. It's not exactly great news, but it isn't bad news either.

Dr. Ainge exhales. "May I ask a question, Jameson?"

She asks questions all the time, but she never asks permission first. I lick my lips, stalling for time, then nod.

She leans forward in her seat. "How did you know the JICC was broken?"

I raise my eyebrows in surprise. "Because we found a part missing after Astra dismantled it."

"And why did she dismantle it?"

"Because I hadn't heard from Dad! We even used that book you gave me." I realize that Dr. Ainge couldn't have loaned me that book at a more fortunate time. I eye her suspiciously. "It's almost like you *knew* the JICC was going to stop working."

"And how would I have known?" she asks.

I consider that, then shrug. "I don't know," I admit. "But you did know—didn't you?"

She leans back in her seat, neither confirming nor denying. "Our brains are trained to hunt for reasons, to make order out of chaos. You might say it's human instinct. We catch a glimpse of someone's face and assign it an identity, and every time a cloud floats by, we feel compelled to name its shape—rabbit, asteroid, what have you. But when our perception doesn't match up with reality, we must be wary of trusting our instincts without question." She looks me in the eyes. "Am I getting through to you?"

I haven't got the slightest clue what this speech has been about, but I force myself to nod. If she thinks you don't understand, she'll keep trying to explain.

Dr. Ainge studies my face. "You seem troubled."

Do I look as vacant on the outside as I feel on the inside? "I do?" I ask, blinking.

"Is there something on your mind?"

I rack my brains for an answer. It doesn't have to be the truth; it just has to be something. "When I saw Astra just now, she acted like she barely knew me."

She folds her arms across her desk. "Correct me if I'm wrong, but I was under the impression that last night was a turning point."

"A turning point?" I ask. Whoever said it was a turning point? "Is that what Astra said?"

"You know I can't discuss one patient's session with another."

I cross my arms across my chest. "Well, then maybe this patient doesn't want to discuss anything, period."

She doesn't take my bait. "Friendships change," she says instead. "They adapt to changing circumstances. But just because they change doesn't mean they stop."

I don't bother to answer. But for once, I hope she's right.

# 18

I VOW TO TALK TO ASTRA sometime during morning break. I never got a chance in class, so I've been planning what to say all morning. Basically I'm going to steal Dr. Ainge's best one-liners.

But as soon as the bell rings, Astra leaps out of her seat and disappears into the hall. I trip over my desk in my rush to follow her, but by the time I reach the door, she's already out of sight. I usually spend breaks in Ms. Pearson's open lab—she programmed the bio-lock with her DNA *and* mine so I can drop in whenever—but then I spot Astra making her way to the gym and head that way instead.

The hall is packed with bodies—the older kids use morning break as a passing period—but I don't need to see to navigate Eleazer Wheelock Ripley. I veer right at the drinking fountain, then slide along the wall until I reach the kindergartners' rooms, ignoring the locker knobs that poke into my ribs along the way.

My nose knows I've reached the gym long before my eyes can see past everyone's shoulders and backpacks. Since no one goes outside unnecessarily these days, the gym has captured—and fermented—ten years' worth of puke and sweat.

"Hey, Jameson!" a bright voice shouts. At first I hope it's Astra's, but it's only Evelyn's. "What are you doing down in Sweatytown? Fifth graders have P.E. on Tuesdays and Thursdays, right?"

I scan the sea of bobbing heads swirling around the busy gym. This would be so much easier if everyone would just hold still. "Oh, you know," I say, scratching the back of my head, "I just need to talk to . . . someone."

"Someone in particular?" she asks. "Or will any launchie do?"

Just then I spot my target on the far side of the gym. Astra's eyes are locked on me, just like mine are now locked on her. "Her," I say emphatically. "I need to talk to *her*."

Evelyn follows my gaze. "What do you want with that complainer?"

Before I have a chance to answer, Astra ducks behind a post,

"Good question," I reply as I take off after her.

Astra is surely better at playing hide-and-seek than I am, but for once I'm more determined. When she hides under the playground for the pint-sized kindergartners, I spot her through the cargo net, and when she hops onto a treadmill, she can't blend into the crowd. But when she disappears into the gravball arena, I lose her for real.

"Astra!" I shout after her, but the gym is so noisy that I'm sure no one can hear me.

No one except for Evelyn, who's apparently been tailing me.

"Hey, Ivan!" she hollers. "Grab the runaway, will you?"

I don't know who Ivan is or how he could possibly know who Evelyn is talking about, but when I step through the portal into the spectator ring, the first thing I see is Astra. She's traded her shoes for a pair of low-grav boots, but a much taller boy, presumably Ivan, has her much shorter arms pinned. They don't stay that way for long. As soon as he lowers his guard, Astra head butts him in the chest.

Ivan swears. "Why'd you do that?"

Astra makes a break for the arena proper, but she doesn't get far before Evelyn tackles her from behind.

"Stand down," Evelyn growls as she struggles to keep Astra pinned. "Jameson just wants to talk."

"And what if I don't want to talk?"

"Too bad," Evelyn says.

Worry bubbles in my stomach as Evelyn drags Astra to her feet. It's like she's reverted to the angry, hostile Astra who moved here a month ago. What in the universe did Dr. Ainge tell her?

"There," Evelyn says once Astra is mostly upright. She tips her head at me. "Your turn."

I feel the heat crawl up my neck as I survey the swarm of onlookers. Six or seven people are crowded around the portal, and everyone in the arena is now pressed up against the steel lattice, hovering at various heights. Their low-grav boots hum expectantly. I don't want to have this talk in front of an audience, but I can't pass up this opportunity.

"I just wanted to say I didn't mean for you to get in trouble—or for your dad to get in trouble. And I'm sorry we got caught." I pause to gauge Astra's reaction, but she's still just standing there scowling. Bravely I forge ahead. "But I'm not sorry we tried."

Two dozen pairs of eyes zoom in on Astra, who digs her toe into a crack in the rubber-tiled floor.

"Well, I'm sorry," she whispers. "I'm sorry we were ever friends."

At first my brain can't process what Astra just said. Even as the words start to sink in—the crowd's gasp speeds things along—I still can't comprehend what she's trying to tell me.

Astra must sense my confusion, because she leans in and whispers, "I said, 'I'm sorry we were ever friends.'" She rips her arm out of Evelyn's grip. "There, I talked. Satisfied now?"

Evelyn ignores her, setting her sights on me instead. "Are you all right, little man?"

I nod, then shake my head. Shake my head, then nod. I don't know what I am. If this is how it feels to have your best friend turn on you, I never want another one.

Astra ducks her head, and for a second, maybe less, I think she's going to come clean, explain herself, take it all back. But the second passes without comment, and she doesn't take it back, just adjusts her twisted shirt and calmly walks away.

This time Evelyn lets her go. "Shake it off, little man," she says. "I'm sure Astra will come around."

Clearly she doesn't know how long Astra can stay upset.

# 19

MOM ISN'T THERE when I get home from my train wreck of a day, so I grab a sleeve of crackers and take shelter in my room. It's already shadowed with twilight, so even though Mom says we shouldn't use the program's power until it's absolutely necessary, I turn on the light. The JICC's deconstructed receiver—router, superhet, translator—sparkles dully, a rough diamond. The monitor reflects the cracker crumbs still clinging to my lips as I power up the rest.

I don't realize I'm nervous until the monitor blinks back to life and there are no waiting messages. The air rushes out of me in one big whoosh; it's now been twelve days since Dad's last transmission. But I should have seen that coming. While the JICC can transmit messages without a receiver, it can't actually receive them.

Sighing, I lean back in my seat and set my sights on the window. There's no activity at Astra's, but a food delivery truck is making its way up the street. I watch the driver drop the ration boxes off at the Coopers' and the Nashes'. Then, when I get bored, I wake the monitor back up and type in UPLOAD with one finger.

"Hey, Dad," I say blithely once the interface pops up. "Just wanted to see how you were doing. The JICC's been having a few problems—nothing serious, don't worry—but Astra and I think we can fix it if we get a new SAFe card."

The thought of Astra makes me frown. Now that we're no longer speaking, I don't know how we'll fix the JICC. I guess we'll have to cross that wormhole once we finally come to it.

I'm still thinking about her when the side door wheezes open, then clicks softly shut again. I send the JICC a sideways glance. The last thing I want to do is make Mom lose it again.

"Looks like I've got to go," I mumble without looking at the screen. "More to follow. Earth to Dad."

I click out of the interface, and the screen dissolves to black. Then I just sit there waiting, counting each one of my breaths. I consider getting up, but then Mom will know I'm here, so I just listen to the squeaks of her shoes on the linoleum. The groans and thuds of cabinets being opened, then pushed shut. I know I should go and help her put away our weekly rations, but I'm too scared to confront her. Too unsure of where we stand.

I sit very still instead and keep an eye on Astra's house, but no one comes or goes. The blinds don't even twitch. I guess they're avoiding me, just like I'm avoiding Mom.

* * *

Sometime later that night, after Mom thinks I'm asleep, she tiptoes into the bathroom and calls someone on her commie. I know it's Mr. Primm when her voice gets high and flirty, but it only takes a minute for her tone to turn angry.

I'm tempted to roll over and stuff my head under my pillow. If they're setting up a date, I don't want to get involved. But Mr. Primm *is* Astra's dad, and Astra *is* my ex-best friend. What if they're talking about *us*?

"—what's going on," Mom is saying when I crack open my door. "It's like they've been joined at the hip, and now they won't talk to each other."

*Are* they talking about us?

"Yes, I know," Mom says abruptly, "and I really can appreciate where Astra's coming from. But it isn't like I'm asking her to outright *lie* to him."

They're definitely talking about us. But what does Mom mean, "*lie* to him"?

I'm still trying to decide when Mom snorts and asks, "Oh no? Because it sure as heck sounds like it."

I wince despite myself. Mr. Primm has no idea what kind of minefield he's walked into. But before Mom has a chance to really get her dander up, she sets it back down and sighs.

"I know," she says. "I *know*. And I need to do it soon."

What does she need to do soon? Hearing only one end of this chat is maddening.

"In the meantime, I'm just asking her to be his friend," Mom says.

I feel my shoulders slump. That's what I want too, but not because Mom forced her.

"Where do we go from here?" Mom asks.

An uncomfortable silence settles over the bathroom as Mr. Primm answers her question. I shift my weight onto one foot, and the floorboards creak deceitfully. I tense my tired muscles, ready to spring back into bed, but Mom doesn't check on me. She must be so deep in thought that she didn't even hear.

I'm about to shift my weight again when Mom smacks the counter in triumph. "That's brilliant, Carl. So brilliant. Then they'll have no choice *but* to talk."

What are they going to do, send Astra and me into the desert with a canteen and a compass? Survival friendships only work if both people make it through.

"So do you have any ideas?"

I can't help but hold my breath, but Mom replies, "No, that's all right. Just let me know what you decide." After a brief pause, she replies, "Same to you, Carl. Good night."

I ease my door shut again and carefully climb back into bed. I'm not sure what they've come up with, but if Mom thinks they can force Astra to do *anything*, she's about to be mistaken.

# 20

I SPEND THE NEXT DAY waiting for Mom to confess her evil plan, but the confession never comes. Not before school and not after. Not when we eat dinner and not when I go to bed. By Friday morning, we're two strangers who bumble around the kitchen and avoid each other's eyes. I honestly don't know how much longer I can take the silence when, amazingly, Mom breaks.

"I've been thinking about picking up an extra shift tomorrow."

I set my toast down with a whack. "We haven't talked for, like, three days, and you want to talk about your *job*?"

"Actually," Mom says, "I want to talk about tomorrow. I've been chatting with Carl—"

"Finally the truth comes out," I mutter.

"—and he asked me to invite you on their trip to Murphyville." She blinks. "What did you say?"

"I said, finally the truth comes out."

She blinks again. "You overheard."

"You *were* yelling," I reply.

Mom doesn't contradict me, just keeps buttering her toast. Hester Dibble fills the silence, blathering on about the launch and what the members of the *Juan Ponce de Léon* are planning to sneak onto the spaceship. Jean Kozlowski says her Kindle. Edom Lev says his son's binky.

Finally Mom dusts off her hands and comes to sit next to me. "Carl and I just want to help." She says it like they're the good guys, like she and *Carl* only have my and Astra's best interests at heart. "I could tell you were upset, and it sounds like she is too."

"Why is she upset?" I ask. "*She's* the one who ditched *me*."

Mom tries—and fails—to hold my gaze. "Maybe it isn't that simple."

"Yeah, well, maybe it should be." I can tell she's hiding something, but I'm in no mood to drag it out of her. I jam my toast into my mouth and chuck my plate into the sink. "I'm going to be late."

Mom's eyes cut to the clock. It's 7:33, so she knows as well as I do that I'm actually early. Still, she doesn't argue—a small victory, at least.

I put on my solar jack, then my backpack, and hurry out the door. I don't stop hurrying until I get past Branislav, so by the time I get to school, I'm a full ten minutes early. After pausing by the office, I veer off toward the open lab. Since Ms. Pearson's at Fort Knox to get recertified or something, it's technically *not* open, but it always is for me.

After letting myself in and easing the door closed on my heels, I set my sights on my workbench. I don't have a ton of time, so I decide to have some fun with the liquid nitrogen. Who doesn't like freezing things, then watching them shatter? I bet Astra does.

I'm still dragging out the canister when the door swings open. Annoyed, I glance over my shoulder—I should have locked the stupid thing—but I freeze when I spot Astra. Our eyes meet and hold across the rows of stained workbenches. Her eyes are blank, as usual, and I can only imagine what mine look like. Worried. Hopeful. Scared.

I've never been good at staring contests—I think I have rapid-eye movement even when I'm awake—so I look away first and make a beeline for the door. But the gap between the workbenches is narrow at best, and Astra doesn't try to move. When I lean the wrong way, our shoulders accidentally bump.

"Sorry," I mumble.

Astra rolls her eyes. "Why are *you* apologizing?"

"Because I bumped you," I reply. "And because, you know, I exist."

"You know, I never said I didn't want you to exist." More softly she adds, "I never even said I didn't want to be your friend."

I sit down on the floor. "You said you wished we never were."

Astra sits down beside me. "No, I said I was sorry I couldn't be a better one."

"There is no way you said that."

"Well, that's what I meant," she says.

I don't know what to say to that, so I don't say anything. When I lean back against the workbench, the test tubes in the attached cabinet swiftly rattle their complaints.

Astra's eyes light up. She gets down on her hands and knees and proceeds to ram her shoulder into the cabinet. "So how much force do we think we have to apply to initiate a chain reaction?"

The first rack of test tubes topples, which knocks over the second rack. And the third rack. And the fourth.

I feel the blood drain from my cheeks—when Ms. Pearson gets back from Fort Knox, she's going to reprogram the bio-lock—but Astra smiles wolfishly.

"Let's check out the spill pattern," she says as she scrambles to her feet.

"No, let's leave them," I hiss, lunging after her, but she's faster than I am. I hit the floor with a splat, squeezing the breath out of my lungs.

"Ouch," Astra says as she rummages around in the cabinet. When I just lie there, not breathing, she looks up long enough to pat me on the back. "Deep breaths. There you go. Get those lungs pumping again."

Though my lungs still feel like used-up whoopee cushions, I try to draw a deep breath, and to my surprise, they inflate. While I push myself back up onto my knees, Astra sits back on her haunches and surveys her handiwork.

"What do you think?" she asks.

I couldn't care less about the state of the cabinet, but for the sake of our friendship, I force myself to sneak a peek. Just as I suspected, the test tubes are a mess. Half of them aren't in their racks, and a third are chipped or broken, but the rest spell out a message: SORRY 2.

I tilt my head to the side. "What's SORRY TWO?" I ask. "Is it, like, some sort of ship?"

"Not T-W-O, you moron. T-O-O! As in 'I'm also sorry.'" Astra lowers her gaze. "I know I've been acting like a jerk."

The back of my throat tightens, but I will *not* cry. "Then why'd you say those awful things?"

She thinks about that for a minute, then mutters, "Because I thought my dad wasn't gonna let me be your friend."

The way she says it makes me wonder if it's true. "So my mom *made* him change his mind?"

"She didn't make him," Astra says. This time it sounds like she means it. "She just helped us . . . understand."

I look down at my toes. I can choose to hold a grudge—against Mom, Astra, the world—or I can let my anger go. I can get my best friend back.

Astra cranes her neck to get a good look at my face. "Best friends again?" she asks.

No sooner has she asked than I know just what I want. "Best friends *always*," I reply.

We clean up in silence, Astra sorting and me shelving. I chuck the broken test tubes into the recycler and use Ms. Pearson's key to grab a fresh supply out of the storage room. While Astra rips off the cellophane and slides the new test tubes into the empty slots, I leave a note for Ms. Pearson apologizing for the mess and offering to work off the cost. I'm adding the finishing touches when Astra comes up behind me.

"You should let me work it off," she says, reading over my shoulder.

I shrug. "It's no big deal. Besides, I already know Ms. Pearson's filing system."

"Well, then you should come with us to Murphyville tomorrow so I can make it up to you."

Murphyville is the small town that sits eight miles to the south. A few years ago, my class took a field trip to Murphy's Grand Menagerie, home of the world's last polar bear, but Mom refused to let me go. She claimed that Murphyville was full of good-for-nothing thieves and terrorists. I guess she's changed her mind.

I feel my insides shrink. "Did my mom put you up to this?"

"What?" Astra asks. "Of course not!" When I arch an eyebrow, her shoulders hunch. "All right, a little. But *I* was the one who picked the Third Rock Galleria."

"What's the Third Rock Galleria?"

Astra's eyes widen. "Wait, you've never been to the Third Rock Galleria? Now you *have* to come. It's like a traveling carnival. Except it doesn't actually travel."

"Oh," I say uncertainly. The thought of leaving Base Ripley is still a little overwhelming, but now that we're talking again, I never, ever want to stop. "All right, then, count me in."

# 21

WHEN I WAKE UP on Saturday, I feel as nauseous as a launchie after his first trip on the centrifuge. I bolt to the bathroom, but nothing comes up. Still, I don't go back to bed, just curl up on the bath mat, since I don't trust my insides.

I've just started to doze when Mom taps on the door. "Jameson, are you OK?"

"I'm fine," I say reflexively before I remember where I am—on the floor, in the bathroom.

I must not fool Mom, because she rattles the doorknob. "Are you decent?" she asks.

I glance down at myself. "Yeah."

"Then I'm coming in," she says as the door starts to swing open. I could have sworn I locked the door, but moms are clever creatures.

Mom gives me a once-over, then whips out the thermometer and runs it across my forehead. After checking the results, she turns the thermometer around so I can see them for myself: 98.2 degrees.

I shrug dismissively. "The calibration could be off."

She runs it across her own forehead and lets me check the results: 98.9 degrees. "And I feel perfectly normal."

"Well, according to this gizmo, you're point-three degrees *above* normal."

Mom slugs me in the shoulder, then looks me in the eyes. "You don't have to go, you know."

"Oh, I want to go," I say, hugging my knees against my chest. "I'm just not sure I want to *leave*."

I haven't left the base since Mom and I moved onto it. Before Astra showed up, I had no desire to. Now I don't know what I want, or at least what I want *most*.

Mom gets down next to me, and even though she doesn't speak, I swear I can hear her thinking, *I could come with you, if you want.*

The offer is tempting—until I imagine what we'd look like in the Third Rock Galleria. Like Mom and Carl are together. Like we're one big, happy family.

Mom squeezes my shoulder. "I could call Dr. Ainge," she says.

Stubbornly I shake my head. "No, I can do it. I *will* do it." Besides, even if we called, I know exactly what she'd say: *Sometimes, Jameson, we have to face what we're afraid of.*

Mom gives my knee a pat. "Well, then we'd better get some breakfast." As she strides out of the bathroom, she adds over her shoulder, "We don't want you to be late!"

The carpet prickles my bare feet as I stumble out of the bathroom, and as I drag my hand along the wall to keep from accidentally falling over, the texturized surface scratches the blisters on my palms. The bumps feel foreign but significant, like Braille I can't quite read.

When I finally reach the kitchen, I have to squint against the sun. Mom is standing at the stove, tending a pot of barleymeal. I choke it down because she took the time to make it for me—and because I don't want her to decide I'm too sick to go after all. I'm still working on the last few bites when someone knocks on the door.

"They're already here?" I blurt as I make a beeline for my room. You can see the dining table from the front door, and the last thing I want to do is be seen in my pajamas.

I'm elbow-deep in my sock drawer when the house makes that sucking sound it makes when someone opens the front door. Mom says something to Astra, and Astra says something back, but their voices can't compete with the gushing in my ears. After triple-checking that I'm not putting them on backward, I stuff my legs into some pants, then yank a shirt over my head. At least my hair is short enough that I can leave it undone.

"Don't you look nice?" Mom asks as I careen into the living room.

This is Mom's way of saying, *Congratulations, son. You put your pants on the right way.* Still, I check them one more time before I slide my arms into the solar jack she's holding out for me.

"Don't forget to bring me a brochure!" she adds as I step onto the porch.

Guilt washes over me like a stink bomb—it's not too late to invite her—but instead of turning back, I pull the door shut behind me. I can only deal with one stressor at a time.

If Astra noticed my hesitation, she's kind enough not to mention it. "Sorry we're late," she says as we tromp across dead grass to the Primms' Electrocar. "Janus thought now would be a good time to experiment with underwear."

"No worries," I reply as I climb into the backseat. Janus does smell like urine, but I don't cover my nose.

Astra's eyes narrow. "We wanted to get an early start, since it's supposed to be less crowded." Under her breath she adds, "So much for less crowded now."

This comment sounds vaguely ominous, but before I can ask her what she means, Mr. Primm says, "Sir Jameson!" like he hasn't seen me in ages and pretends to doff his cap. "We thank thee for the privilege of escorting thee to Murphyville."

I can't help but grin. "I probably should be thanking *thee*."

He gestures toward the passenger seat. "Are you sure you don't want to ride up here? I'm sure this fair maiden wouldn't mind riding in the back."

Astra glares, but I can't tell if it's because of what he called her or because she doesn't want to switch seats. Either way I don't push it. "Oh no, that's all right," I say. "I like staring at headrests."

One corner of Astra's mouth curls up, and suddenly I feel a little better.

Mr. Primm just shrugs. "As you wish," is all he says as he backs out of the driveway. The engine splutters like a dragon that's just been rudely awakened, but at least it doesn't protest when Mr. Primm punches the gas.

I watch our houses fade from view. I swear I can see Mom watching *us* from the window in the living room, her pinched lips and worried eyes getting smaller and smaller. My stomach growls at me again, but I force the nausea back down. The last thing I want to do is add another odor to the mix.

When we turn onto Aldrin Way, I stick my head between my knees, but that just makes me dizzier, so I force myself to look back up. The guardhouse is dead ahead, but Branislav doesn't make us stop, just waves Mr. Primm right through.

"What's the first thing you want to see when we get there?" Mr. Primm asks.

"The sidewalk," I mumble. I just want to get out of this car.

He meets my gaze in the rearview, and even Astra takes a moment to sneak a peek over her shoulder. Uncomfortable, I look away and lean my head against the window, which is still a little cool.

Mr. Primm glances at Astra, then launches into a long monologue about the First Crusade. He's still going on about Pope Urban and capturing Constantinople when she sneaks another peek over her shoulder. From the way she rolls her eyes, I can tell that this performance is supposed to be distracting me. I can't decide whether I feel more grateful or annoyed.

I wedge my fist under my chin and let Mr. Primm's rich baritone sink into my brain. It sounds nothing like Dad's voice, but I'm kind of glad it doesn't. This voice doesn't erase any of Dad's stories in my head, just lays new ones down beside them.

I don't realize I've closed my eyes until they fly open again. Somehow we've reached the main gate. My memories of this place are fuzzy and indistinct, so I sit up a little straighter. The heavy-gauge chain-link is familiar, but it was taller in my memory. The guardhouse seemed taller too, and if the fence was ever topped with curlicues of barbed wire, it isn't anymore.

The Marines in the guardhouse make Mr. Primm roll down his window, but all he has to do is show them his tag and explain where we're going. The Marine at his window, a scrawny-looking guy with fatigues that look too big for him, nods to the one in the guardhouse, and the main gate swings open. Mr. Primm nods at both Marines, then pushes back down on the gas.

My head swivels around like a broken antenna as we roar away from Base Ripley. I've never seen so much earth and sky in the same place. As the main gate shuts behind us, my stomach finally settles down, and it feels like I'm flying, or maybe falling, toward the sky.

Once the main gate is far behind us, I set my sights on the window. The little clumps of dirt edging the road whip by so fast I can't possibly count them, but the sand dunes pass more slowly, and the distant clouds look like they're not moving at all.

Mr. Primm catches my eye in the rearview. "When was the last time you went to Murphyville?" he asks. He has to shout the question, since his window is rolled down, but the way his hand is gliding up and over the air currents has me completely mesmerized.

"Uh, never?" I reply as I keep staring at his hand. I want to roll my window down and make my hand glide through the air, but I'm too afraid to try.

Astra whips around. "You've *never* been to Murphyville?"

"Well, I've been there once," I say, sticking my chin out for good measure.

"When you first moved here?" she asks.

I press my lips into a line. If I don't answer her question, then she'll never know for sure.

Mr. Primm bats that away. "Who cares how many times you've been to Murphyville?" he asks. "The most important thing is that we're going there today—and that we'll be together."

I like the sound of that.

# 22

I CLEARLY DON'T DO ROAD TRIPS, so I'm not exactly sure how long it takes to drive eight miles. It doesn't *seem* like it should take long, but I'm still surprised when manmade structures start popping up along the road. At first they whiz by so fast I can't get a good look at them, but it isn't long before they're big enough to sink my eyes into.

The first building of any size is a two-story structure made of weathered wooden boards that have been nailed tightly together. The place next door is only one story, but it's made of the same wooden boards. It's not until I see a woman coming out of the third one that I realize what these buildings are: houses. I've never seen a neighborhood with houses that look different from each other.

When Mr. Primm stops at the first intersection, I press my nose against the glass. There's a commissary on one corner and a Laundromat across from it. Judging by the weighed-down clothesline stretching across a nearby alley, I'd say it's a real Laundromat, with real washing machines that wash real people's clothes. Except the windows have strange signs: *HALF OFF HAIRCUTS* one declares. *BROCCOLI $8.99/LB* another claims.

"What's that funny-looking S with the line down the middle?" I ask Astra as her dad makes a right turn. "And why do they want to give us half a haircut?"

Astra looks over her shoulder, not at me but at the signs. "Oh, that's a dollar sign," she says, which doesn't mean anything to me. "And they don't want to give you half a haircut. They're saying you can *buy* a haircut for half of its normal cost."

"What does that mean, 'you can buy a haircut'?"

Before Astra can answer, Mr. Primm replies, "It's how you obtain goods and services out here. You go out and get a job, your boss pays you for your work, and you turn around and buy stuff like bread and haircuts."

That sounds like a stupid system. "What if you run out?" I ask.

"Of haircuts?"

"Of money."

"Well, then you have to do more work."

"How much money do you get?"

Mr. Primm shifts in his seat. "It varies from job to job, but from what I understand, the going rate in Murphyville is twenty dollars an hour."

"But you can barely buy two pounds of broccoli for that!"

Astra props her elbow on the armrest and plops her chin into her hand. "We're not on the base anymore, Toto."

I'm still processing this information when we make another turn and a sparkling white building appears around the corner. It's three stories tall and made of alabaster stone with a central dome that makes it look like an observatory and three rows of narrow windows. The windows must have been designed to let in as little light as possible, which means this building was built *after* the asteroid ruined everything. I don't know a word to describe the building as a whole, but when Janus calls it a castle, I decide to go with that.

Mr. Primm throws his arms up as we pull into the parking lot. "Welcome to the Third Rock Galleria! It was built to be the seat of government after Washington, D.C., sank—the New White House, they called it. But after one of the protests got kind of physical—well, violent— President Murphy and his staff relocated to the base."

"Cowards," Astra mutters.

Mr. Primm sends her a sharp look as he shifts into park. "They *weren't* cowards," he replies. "President Murphy wasn't the only one who relocated."

She has no clever comeback to this dig.

A not-so-invisible rain cloud seems to hover over us as we climb out of the car and head into the galleria. A wall of warm air hits us as soon as we step through the door, but at least the toxic sun is no longer beating down on us. The foyer is two stories high, with marble floors, dark wooden railings, and a sun-shaped chandelier that's almost as bright as the real thing. At least whoever built this place also had a sense of humor.

Mr. Primm greets the old man sitting behind the ticket desk. On one corner is a sign that says *ADMISSION: $30*, and on the other is a sign that says *PRICES NEGOTIABLE.*

"We'll take four tickets," he says as he pulls out his leather wallet.

The old man presses some buttons on an ancient-looking tablet. "That will be two hundred dollars."

Mr. Primm nods at the sign. "Isn't it thirty a pop?"

"Not for Ripleys," the old man says.

I glance down at my solar jack. How can he tell we're from the base? It isn't like we have *BASE RIPLEY* stenciled somewhere on our backs.

Mr. Primm nods at the other sign. "Aren't prices negotiable?"

"Yes," the old man says. "For Murphys."

Sighing, Mr. Primm withdraws a wad of these magical dollars and passes them to the old man. I'm not sure how he knows how many dollars to give him, but Mr. Primm must get it right, because the old man takes his money, slides it into a metal drawer, and holds up a rubber stamp.

"No tickets," he explains as he stamps our hands in turn and gives Mr. Primm a sack of tokens. "We don't cut trees down around here."

"Good for you," Mr. Primm says. "And thank you for your assist—"

"Hey," the old man interrupts, waggling his bushy eyebrows. "Don't I know you from somewhere?"

If having a dead parent makes you famous on Base Ripley, it must make you practically a demigod out here. But before I have a chance to formally introduce the Primms, Astra leans across the desk.

"Sorry, old man," she replies after inspecting his features, "but I'm one-hundred-percent sure I've never seen you in my life."

The old man starts to reply, but Mr. Primm whisks us away before he can say another word.

"Hey!" the old man hollers. "Don't you want to check your jackets?"

Mr. Primm doesn't slow down. "We'll wear them!" he hollers back.

I glance back just in time to see the old man throw up his arms. I can't help but grin. I would have preferred to leave my solar jack with him, but I still like the idea of doing something bold and daring.

We pound up the sweeping staircase, taking the steps two at a time. Janus is giggling like a wind-up toy, and even our resident rain cloud is trying to suppress a smile. Mr. Primm, our fearless leader, is cackling like a wicked witch—until we turn a random corner and almost crash into a worker.

Astra and I skid to a stop, but Janus doesn't even slow. Mr. Primm scoops him off his feet just before he makes contact.

"My apologies," he says, sounding like a teenage troublemaker instead of a grown-up dad.

The worker doesn't answer, just glares at each of us in turn. I study my shoes, too embarrassed to meet her gaze.

Mr. Primm waits for the worker to stick her nose in the air and disappear into a side room, then sets Janus back down. "I think we'll be less conspicuous if we walk from here."

At the top of the staircase, I get my first real glimpse of the Third Rock Galleria. It's a wonder to behold. The floor we're standing on has become a balcony, with marbled pillars for support and a gilded railing for safety. Arcade games line the balcony, but the galleria's centerpiece is the double-decker carousel down on the first floor. I've heard of carousels, of course, but I've never seen one in real life. The mint-green roof and white supports remind me of a birthday cake.

Mr. Primm motions toward the nearest game, something called Skee-Ball. "Want to take it for a spin?"

Astra doesn't answer him, so I take the lead instead.

"Can Astra and I explore a little on our own?" I ask. "I promise we won't hurt anything."

Mr. Primm's smile is sad. "I'm not worried about *you* hurting anything in *here*." Under his breath he adds, "Quite the opposite, in fact."

I'm not sure what he means, but I'm not sure I want to ask.

He surveys the balcony, which is virtually empty, then blows out a gusty sigh. "Don't talk to strangers, don't touch anything you know you're not supposed to"—he hands me the sack of tokens—"and *don't* forget to meet back here at eleven thirty sharp."

"We won't!" I say eagerly, tugging Astra toward the games. I don't want him to change his mind.

The galleria is a maze of bells and whistles and distractions, so I'm content to drift at first, my head tipped back like an antenna. Base Ripley was designed with a single goal—survival—so I've never seen so many things that serve no practical purpose. But then we come across one very specific game, and I know we have to stop.

"Whack-an-Alien!" I say.

"So it is," Astra replies. She doesn't sound very impressed.

I grip the console with both hands. "I've always wanted to play this!" Dad's described the old version, an awesome game called Whack-a-Mole. Now that I think about it, though, he never did tell me what a mole was.

Astra shrugs. "Knock yourself out."

She parks herself on a short bench while I retrieve the rubber mallet and feed the slot a grubby token. Then the invasion begins.

I'm in the middle of round nine when I happen to look up and spot a pair of gawking girls. They're not exactly watching us, but every time I look at them, they quickly look away. A shiver skitters down my spine, until I remind myself that they're not interested in me, that they're interested in Astra.

"I heard there's a drinking fountain underneath the balcony." I say it way too loud, but the gawking girls don't seem to find it strange at all. "We should go and get a drink."

I have no idea whether or not there's a drinking fountain, but Astra lets me steer her toward the stairs in the corner. As we put some distance between us and our not-so-secret admirers, I feel a weight slide off my chest— until I spot the gawking girls, who have clearly followed us.

My stomach does a somersault. It's not like they're with UNN, so they probably won't try to talk, but they might take Astra's pic. Paying teenagers for pics of famous grieving families seems like just the sort of trick that Davis Darwin would resort to.

I pretend to check my commie. "Isn't it time to meet your dad?"

Astra cocks an eyebrow at me—I asked the question ten times louder than I really needed to—but at least the gawking girls retreat. "He didn't say we had to meet him until—"

"Right now!" I cut in as I shove her behind a pillar. If those gawking girls can't see us, maybe they'll give up and leave.

"What are you doing?" Astra hisses as she bats my hands away.

"Did you see those gawking girls?" I ask.

"How could I miss them?" she replies.

I cup a hand around my mouth. "I don't mean to alarm you, but I think they're tailing you."

Astra shakes her head. "They're probably tailing *you* as much as they're tailing me."

"What do you mean by that?" I ask.

Astra stiffens momentarily. "Never mind," she says with a slick flick of her wrist. "Pretend that I never said anything."

"But you *did* say something," I reply.

"And then I said, '*Never mind.*'" She forces me out of the way. "Let's leave those bozos in our dust."

Even though it was my idea, I have to hurry to keep up. The noise fades momentarily as we descend the darkened stairs, then hits us again full force once we reach the lower floor. I'm still itching to ride that double-decker carousel, but as we turn another corner, Astra shudders to a stop.

Ten or twenty feet away, next to something called a scrambler, Mr. Primm has been surrounded by a gaggle of old women. They look like harmless grandmas, but Mr. Primm keeps backing up, like he's anxious to escape. When one of the old ladies offers him a scrap of paper, he holds up both hands.

"Thank you," he half says, half shouts, "but I don't want to date your daughter."

I don't have a chance to process the small spike of jealousy that's suddenly rippling through my veins before a greasy-looking man shoves a grandma out of his way.

"Get out of Murphyville!" he shouts. "Who said we wanted you here, Primm?"

# 23

I MUST HAVE MISUNDERSTOOD. That's the only explanation. But then the grandmas start to whisper, and I know I heard him right.

Mr. Primm bends down to scoop Janus off the dusty floor. His methodical movements don't match the multicolored lights flashing frantically behind him. "I'm sorry you feel that way, sir. It wasn't our intention to offend."

"Your *existence* offends, Primm. It just reminds us of the difference between the haves and the have-nots."

Mr. Primm keeps his face smooth. "If you have a concern, you should take it up with the program."

"Oh right, the *program*," the man says. He makes it sound like a dirty word. "Yes, I'm sure they'll take the time to come down from their ivory tower to address the likes of *me*."

This bozo makes it sound like the program is picking and choosing who to save and who to throw into the sun. But they're trying to save *everyone*.

Instead of correcting the man's ignorance, Mr. Primm surveys the crowd. I start to work my way toward him, towing Astra along with me, but when he catches my gaze, he gently shakes his head. I shudder to a halt, confused. Does he want us to come or stay?

"What are you doing?" the man asks. "Looking for a friendly face? You won't find any around here."

Mr. Primm pays him no heed. He cocoons Janus in his arms and keeps his eyes trained on the floor. Dad would have stood his ground, forced the man to take it back, but as I watch Mr. Primm work his way around the crowd, showing respect, demanding none, a part of me can't help but wonder if his way's the better way.

But the man's not finished yet. "Then again," he says, "maybe the program's *not* the problem. Maybe the problem is you Primms. How stupid do you have to be to get crushed by *anything* at thirty-seven-percent gravity?"

A white-hot lightning bolt zigzags across my field of vision. Did he just call Dr. Primm stupid for dying in the line of duty? In front of her two kids?

The crowd goes uncomfortably still, and even Astra has the good sense not to come out, fists swinging. As I look back and forth between her and Mr. Primm, I know what I have to do. The Primms may not be *my* family, but they're my people, my friends.

"I guess it takes one to know one," I say as loudly as I dare.

The man's eyes roll around in his head, trying to pinpoint his new target. I'm tempted to duck behind the scrambler, but in the end, I hold my ground.

"And you're absolutely right," I add once his eyes are locked on me. Hopefully the man can't hear the tiny tremble in my voice. "If you think the program's going to save someone as stupid as you are, you're going to be disappointed."

Mr. Primm, who's nearly reached us, sends me a warning look, which I pretend not to notice. The man's answering leer is much harder to ignore.

"What's this?" he asks. "A surrogate?" He circles me like a rogue satellite. "I didn't think they came so small."

"Ignore him," Mr. Primm says. "If you've ever trusted me, you'll turn around and walk away."

"Yeah, turn around and walk away." The man gestures grandly toward the exit. "Go ahead and prove me right."

Mr. Primm's eyes are encouraging, and I know I can trust him, but I don't like that man's smirk. He shouldn't be allowed to spread lies about the program or insults about the Primms.

"I'm not a surrogate," I say, but that's mostly just because I don't know what a surrogate *is*.

"Oh yeah?" the man replies. "Then tell us, peanut—what's your name?"

I don't have a chance to answer before Astra grabs my arm and digs her nails into my skin. I force myself not to cry out, since I don't want to give the man any additional ammunition.

"Jameson," I say through gritted teeth. "My name is Jameson O'Malley."

The man rears back as if I've struck him, and the nervous crowd goes still again. I know I've said something wrong, but before I have a chance figure out exactly what, Mr. Primm spins me around.

"I should have known," the man hollers as Mr. Primm hauls us away. "Martian orphans stick together!"

Before I can process that, Mr. Primm grabs hold of my collar and drags me out of view. He won't let me go, and now we're picking up speed, Janus bouncing on his hip. I look around for Astra, but she's fallen into step beside us.

"It's all right," I say once we've turned a dozen corners. I shake off Mr. Primm's grip. "I'm not going to go back."

"Did he hurt you?" he demands as he looks me up and down.

"I'm fine," I say tiredly. That guy might have been a jerk, but he didn't lay a hand on me.

Mr. Primm exhales. "Well, that's something, anyway. Maybe Mina won't *completely* kill me." He sets Janus back down. "Let's blow this Popsicle stand."

I gesture up the hall. "But what about—"

"We're *going*," he growls. When I shrink back, he sighs. "I'm sorry, Jameson, but we don't really have a choice. It's too crowded today."

This corridor is clearly empty, so I don't know what he means. Still, I don't argue, just fall into step behind him. Since we still have our solar jacks, we can escape through a side entrance. I'm momentarily flummoxed by the *EMERGENCY EXIT ONLY* sign, but Mr. Primm just ignores it. If an alarm goes off when he shoves open the door, it's too far away for us to hear.

After spending so much time in a place designed to block it out, the sun seems especially threatening. I double-check my solar jack while Mr. Primm adjusts Janus' hood. Once he's sure it's on snugly, Mr. Primm leads us across the parking lot. No one says anything as we pile back into the car and set a course for home.

The silence gives my brain time to chew on what I heard. Clearly that man hated the program, but what I don't understand is *why*.

"Why did that man get so upset?" I ask as Murphyville goes by in reverse: first the Laundromat, then the commissary, then the mismatched wooden houses.

Mr. Primm's grip tightens. "We live in a complex world," he says. "When that asteroid knocked us out of whack, most people agreed that we should do whatever it took to save our kids and our kids' kids. But there were a few who thought that we should just accept our fate."

"Like the people who protested outside the New White House," I say.

"Yeah, like them," Mr. Primm says.

Silence descends again, giving my brain more time to think, to mull over the man's words. I replay them in my head until I get to the last line, which repeats over and over: *Martian orphans stick together. Martian orphans stick together.*

*Orphans*, as in plural.

I try to clear my throat, but something's definitely stuck. "What did he mean by 'Martian orphans'?" I whisper.

Astra and Mr. Primm exchange a short but heated look. When Mr. Primm just shakes his head, Astra turns the other way and knots her arms across her waist. Neither says a single word.

"Mr. Primm, what did he mean?"

Mr. Primm licks his dry lips. "I'm sorry you had to hear that, Jameson. It isn't a nice term."

I guessed as much from the man's tone, but that wasn't what I asked. "But why'd he even say it? Was he talking about Janus?"

Mr. Primm doesn't reply, just cracks his neck. I don't move a single muscle. I'm afraid that if I do, I'll upset whatever forces are still holding me together. That whatever they *won't* tell me has more pull than what they will.

"*Please*, Mr. Primm," I squeak. "I need to know."

He clenches and unclenches the steering wheel. "It's not my place to tell you."

"Then whose place is it?" I demand.

"I don't know," Mr. Primm admits. "But if it's anyone's, it's Mina's."

The way he says her name, like he and Mom are more than friends, makes me want to throw something out the window. Mr. Primm may be all right, but I do *not* need a new dad.

"What about you?" I ask Astra. She's been watching me in the side mirror, so I know she knows I'm watching her. "Do *you* know what's going on?"

She holds my gaze for a few seconds, then angles the side mirror away.

"Of course you do," I say, incensed. "Apparently everyone does—everyone except for me!"

"Jameson," she says, but Mr. Primm holds up a hand.

"Astra, no. You *can't.*"

"But aren't we kind of lying to—"

"It's not our place," Mr. Primm says.

I lean forward in my seat. The seat belt pulls across my chest. "Astra, *please*," I say. "You can tell me anything. I'm not going to freak out."

Astra squeezes her eyes shut and grips the armrests with both hands. It looks like she's mouthing something, maybe a mantra or a prayer, and I think, I really think, she's going to tell me.

But then I read her lips: *It's not my place. It's not my place. It's not my place. It's not my place.*

Suddenly I wish I could throw *myself* out the window. But I can't, of course. I'm stuck in this backseat, this Electrocar, this life. Besides, the base is visible, so it's not like I'd get far.

It takes the Marines less time to let us in than it did to let us out, but that's probably because they remember Mr. Primm. I unbuckle my seat belt as soon as we hit Wheelock Park, then launch myself out of my seat as soon as we pull into the driveway. But my dramatic exit gets cut short when my toe catches on the doorframe, and I go down, hard, on the concrete.

Astra sits up. "Jameson!" She rips off her own seat belt and gets down on the ground beside me.

"I'm *fine*," I say as I scoot away from her. My foot turned when my toe caught, so I think my ankle's sprained, but there's no way I'm saying that. Astra said that she was sorry, that we'd always be best friends, but she won't tell me the truth.

I'm starting to think that no one will.

Astra grabs my arm. "Let me help you up."

I yank it out of reach. "I can do it by myself."

I try to put weight on my ankle, but it immediately fires off a warning shot: *Nice try, Astra's not-friend, but if you want to get us out of here, you're going to have to do better than that.* That leaves me no choice but to literally drag myself back to my feet using the Electrocar as leverage. My arms burn with the strain, but I refuse to ask for help.

Widening rivers of sweat are carving canyons down my back by the time I'm mostly upright, but I pretend not to notice. I still have to deal with the Herculean task of getting myself to the front door. Every other step is borderline excruciating, but I don't make a sound. I don't want Astra or her dad to know how much I'm struggling.

By the time I make it to the porch, I feel exhausted but triumphant. I did it. By myself. I almost want them to congratulate me, but when I glance over my shoulder, Mr. Primm just dips his head.

At least Astra has the decency to meet my gaze. She looks me right in the eyes when she says, "Your dad is dead. There, I told you. Happy now?"

# 24

YOUR DAD IS DEAD.

*Your dad is dead.*

The words ping-pong around my brain like electrons in a mass spectrometer, bumping, knocking, jostling. I know what each means on its own, but when I try to line them up, they don't want to stay in place:

*Your dead is dad.*

*Is dad your dead.*

I shake my head. "That can't be true. You're lying."

Astra keeps going, going, going. "He knew the JICC wouldn't be ready, he knew it was missing a key part, so he recorded tons of vids before the *Amerigo Vespucci* left."

I press my hands over my ears. I can't handle more words right now. They won't fit inside my brain. They won't fit inside my *life*.

"That's enough!" Mr. Primm says, but Astra must disagree, because her mouth doesn't stop moving.

"Your mom beamed them to the JICC from a transmitter in her closet, and it worked—it worked too well—until the vids finally ran out—"

She doesn't have a chance to finish before Mom flies out of the house. She's screaming something terrible at the top of her lungs, but I can't make out the words. Astra darts around the car, wisely putting it between them, but Mom doesn't quit coming.

Mr. Primm leaps out of his seat just in time to intercept her. "Mina, you have to calm down." When she throws herself at Astra, outstretched fingers curled like claws, he's strong enough to hold her back. "MINA, YOU HAVE TO CALM DOWN!"

At least that snaps her out of it. Mom retracts her claws, but now she's howling like a wolf I once saw on a nature show. The wolf's pups had just been killed by a marauding grizzly bear. I dig my fists into my ears and try to think of something happy, but I can't get the sight of those wolf pups out of my head.

I stumble backward without thinking, tripping over the driveway, then a clump of crunchy grass. I've almost reached the porch when I catch a glimpse of Astra, who's watching me with solemn eyes. *I'm sorry*, they seem to say. *Having a dead parent sucks, right?*

But I don't want Astra's pity, just like she didn't want mine. She can't be right. Of course she can't. I spin away from her and stumble up the concrete steps, forcing my way into the house and the safety of my room.

Mom keeps howling at the sky for what seems like several days. I lower myself into my chair and stare blankly at the homework I didn't quite finish last night. But at the back of my brain, an insistent voice keeps asking, *What if Astra isn't wrong?*

I shake my head to clear it. Imagining that annoying voice getting flung against my skull makes it quiet down a little. I will not give in to doubt. I will *not* give in to doubt.

I don't hear Mom come in, so I don't notice her standing on the threshold of my room until she half breathes, half sobs. I glance over my shoulder, and there she is, the mama wolf. Her eyes are red and splotchy, but her cheeks are splotchier. She didn't wear her solar jack, so the creases from Mr. Primm's are now imprinted on her cheek.

I deflate. "What do you want?"

"To talk," she says quietly.

"What is there to talk about? Astra got some bad info. End of story."

The muscles in Mom's neck ripple. "You think Astra lied to you?"

That insistent voice comes back, chanting, *Astra isn't wrong.* I shake my head again to clear it. "Didn't she?"

Mom tiptoes across the room and lowers herself onto the bed. "When terrible things happen, things that we don't understand, it's normal to push them aside, to want to deal with them later. But pushing them aside doesn't make them go away. Someday we have to face them."

I'm not sure what to make of this little monologue. Mom usually lets Dr. Ainge do the counseling around here.

"I'm *so* sorry," she goes on. Her voice catches in her throat. "You shouldn't have found out like that. I should have told you last week or last month or even right after it happened, but I wasn't thinking straight."

"Right after *what* happened?" I ask.

Mom draws a bracing breath. "It had something to do with the navigational equipment. They were able to reach Mars, but somehow they couldn't land. The angle of entry wasn't right. The president herself showed up at my shadehouse, told me everything at work."

Mom recites these facts like she pulled them out of a book. But even if what she says is true, why should I believe her now? After all, she's apparently spent the past two years lying to my face.

Mom takes my silence as acceptance. "When your dad asked me to upload his prerecorded messages, I really didn't think much of it. Well, I did think it seemed sneaky, but it seemed harmless at the time. At least you'd have *something* to get you through after he left."

I resist the urge to snort. "Don't you mean 'after he blew up'?"

She manages to let this go. "After the crash, I became a wreck myself. I stopped eating. I stopped sleeping. I lost nearly fifteen pounds in that first month and half. The last thing I wanted to do was let it destroy you too. You were so invested in those vids, and since I still had so many . . . I just kept uploading them. Then days turned into weeks, and then weeks turned into months, and I couldn't bring myself to stop . . . until they finally ran out."

The scale of her betrayal is frightening. Still, I decide to play along. Maybe I can get more information. "So what if they hadn't run out? What if Astra hadn't blabbed?"

"I don't know," Mom admits. "But I never meant to hurt you. You have to believe that, Jamie. I was trying *not* to hurt you."

My thoughts are spinning so fast I may as well be on a centrifuge. "How did you hide it for so long?"

Mom looks ashamed. "I told the school I was struggling and asked them not to bring it up. Ms. Cook and Mr. Flores, even your teachers and your classmates—they were happy to agree. Then I asked Dr. Ainge if she would start seeing you to help me prepare you for . . . well, we never got that far. I wasn't ready to tell you, and she had to go along. When I called to tell her I was almost out of vids, she said it was time to come clean, but I didn't know how to do it."

At least that explained the book.

"I'm so sorry. So, so sorry." Mom drags a hand under her nose. "Do you think there's any way you can ever forgive me?"

Can I ever *forgive* her? I'm not even ready to believe her. I keep my mouth firmly shut.

She seems to understand. "OK," she says. Her shoulders slump. "I guess I'll let you process things."

Mom leaves as softly as she came. I let her go without a word. I feel used up, wrung out, like a rain sponge that's run dry. If Mom ran out of messages, maybe I've run out of feelings.

As shadows slither down the walls and spread out across my bed, I keep my eyes trained on the JICC. If it *does* wake up, I'll know for sure that Dad's alive. He's the only one who can access the JICC's feed.

Suddenly *1 NEW TRANSMISSION* pops up on the screen.

I lean forward in my seat. Even though I know Dad won't be able to see me, I comb my fingers through my hair and smooth the wrinkles in my shirt. After drawing a deep breath, I hastily type in *DOWNLOAD*. My pulse thuds in my wrists, drumming steadily against the keyboard, but when the image resolves into a face I recognize, it isn't Dad's.

It's Astra's.

"I know I'm not your dad," she says. I've never set foot in her room, so I'm not sure that's where she is, but the pale gray walls look right. "You probably thought I was. I'm sorry."

I *did* think she was Dad. I can't decide which bugs me more—that I'm so predictable or that she knows me so well.

"I didn't mean to get your hopes up, but I had to talk to you. I doubted you would let me in after what happened earlier, so I tried this route instead. You know, if you'd installed a WAF, I wouldn't have been able to."

I snort despite myself. A web application firewall *would* have blocked this little vid, but then, no one's felt compelled to hack my signal before.

"OK, now I'm just stalling." She wipes her hands off on her pants, which makes me wonder if they're sweaty too. "I wanted to tell you I was sorry for telling you the truth like that . . . and for not telling you before. After we got caught that night at the commissary, my dad told me everything. He said the *Amerigo Vespucci* never actually landed. Their navigational equipment failed, so they had to calculate their vectors or whatever on their own, but they must have messed them up, because they skipped across the atmosphere before they . . . broke apart."

She makes it sound so peaceful, like their spaceship was a stone skipping across a tranquil pond. But atmospheres aren't made of gentle banks and lily pads; they're made of heat and flames and death.

"They sent the *Marco Polo* to recover what they could—and to look for possible survivors. Apparently they found the debris field, but there were no human remains." Astra looks down at her hands. "The four missions they've sent since haven't found anything either."

"Yeah, but were they looking?" I can't help but ask the screen.

"I wanted to tell you right away, but Dad kept saying you were 'fragile.'" She makes air quotes with her fingers. "He said it was our job to respect your mom's decision, even if we disagreed. I didn't think that I could do that, so I stopped hanging out with you. But that was the wrong decision too."

The sadness in her voice makes me want to reach into the monitor and give her shoulder a pat, but as soon as that thought registers, I push it aside. I don't want to feel sympathy for her. I don't want to feel anything right now.

"Anyway," Astra goes on, "I thought you deserved to know the truth. If you ever want to talk for real, you know when and where to find me."

She reaches for the kill switch, and the monitor goes black.

I go back over her message, then the things that Mom told me, searching my memory for clues. Mom *did* lose weight a few years back, but she told me she was sick. That was also her excuse for not watching UNN—she said the loudness hurt her head. I guess those could have been excuses, but they could have been truths too. They certainly made sense at the time.

Groaning without meaning to, I drag myself out of my chair and collapse onto the bed. Mom has turned the wall screen up to deafness-inducing decibels, so I can hear every word coming out of Hester Dibble's mouth. She's going on again about the *Juan Ponce de Léon*.

As she runs through the details like the good anchor she is—"Liftoff is set for March eighteenth at twelve ten in the afternoon"—my memory rewinds to the day Dad blasted off. With its bright white rocket boosters and its shiny silver pod, the *Amerigo Vespucci* was a wonder to behold. I remember how Dad looked—so confident in the coveralls emblazoned with the program's seal—as he stood on the fancy purple carpet they'd rolled out in front. A little scared, mostly eager in the see-through elevator that whisked him up to the pod. Then completely confident again on the catwalk that ushered him to the *Amerigo Vespucci*. He looked so vivid, so *alive*, and as that thought comes together, another thought does too:

*What if Astra isn't* right? *What if Dad's not* really dead?

Astra all but admitted that they never found the bodies, so what if someone—Dad—survived? It's not like they've been looking for him. He could be stranded, all alone, on the other side of Mars. Waiting for someone, *anyone*, to finally come and rescue him.

That's when a rudimentary plan starts to take shape in my head.

# 25

THE NEXT SEVERAL DAYS are a blur of preparation. If I'm going to find Dad and reunite him with two worlds, then I have a lot to do.

First I make a list of all the stuff I'm going to need. Then I try to figure out how I'm going to get it. Some of it is easy to track down. The food delivery trucks always have space food on hand, and since I'm a growing boy, Maury thinks I need a lot when I ask her for some samples.

Some of it is harder, though. Small canisters of oxygen aren't difficult to find, but if I'm going to be living in a vacuumed cargo hold for the next three or four months—the time it will take to get there with Earth and Mars in prime position—then I'm going to go through more than a few gallons of air. I'm also going to require a fully automated space suit, preferably with a built-in waste removal system.

I haven't figured out how to get my hands on that space suit, so I decide to focus on my modes of transportation. Thankfully the hard part's covered—though the crew doesn't know it yet, the *Juan Ponce de Léon* is going to ferry me to Mars. There are always last-minute supplies that need to be loaded, and they aren't usually well guarded. They must think no one would be dumb enough to sneak into the cargo hold. As long as I can smash myself into a cargo canister, I should be good to go.

That said, the portion of the trip from Wheelock Park to the launch site is going to be tricky. After wrecking her Light-Year, I doubt Evelyn will want to do me any more favors. I can probably hitch a ride on an outgoing supply truck, assuming the driver doesn't realize I'm there, but I'm still going to need to get myself to the depot. And *that* means I'm going to need to upgrade the hoverboard.

I get started after dinner. Mom and I have gone back to avoiding one another, so after inserting my plate into the waterless dish sanitizer, I make a break for the garage.

Mom looks up from the peas she's been pushing around her plate. "Where are you going?" she asks.

At first I think the jig is up; she figured out what I've been up to. But as I study her more closely, I realize that she's not mad. If anything, she's curious, like a neighbor might be about your weekend plans.

"Just out to the garage," I say. I think about mentioning the hoverboard, then decide not to push it.

"That's a good idea," she says. "Your lungs can always use fresh air."

I don't think anyone would consider the air out there *fresh*, but I still say, "OK, Mom." Then I slip silently outside.

The garage is the one room Mom hasn't touched since Dad left for Mars. His tool chest hulks in the corner, and the workbench is still cluttered with his junk. I trace the ring of a pop can imprinted on its gritty surface, remembering the many times we burped "Twinkle, Twinkle, Little Star." I swear it still feels slightly sticky.

After wiping off my hand, I heave my hoverboard onto the workbench. The first thing I do is check the existing parts. That's the first rule of building things—always make sure the stuff you build still does what it's supposed to do.

After inspecting the fans, the engine, and the control panel, I set my sights on the capacitor. I added it several years ago to maximize the battery's shelf life, but now I'm more interested in speed. If I'm going to make it to the launch site before the *Juan Ponce de León* lifts off, this hunk of polycarbonate will have to do more than hover. It will have to almost *fly*.

With painstaking precision, I unscrew the now-defunct capacitor and survey my handiwork. I can't help but grunt approvingly as my eyes rove over the wiring, but there's no sense in admiring old work.

I retrieve Dad's wire cutters and am about to snip a yellow wire when an unexpected voice says, "I wouldn't cut that one if I were you."

I glance over my shoulder. Astra's feisty silhouette is perfectly framed in the opening.

"Why not?" I ask too sharply.

She takes a cautious step across the threshold, then, when I don't object, scurries over to the workbench. "Because if you cut that one, your battery's gonna be disabled."

I lean back to get a better look. When I discover that she's right, I press my lips into a line.

"But if you cut *that* one," she says, pointing at a red-and-white-striped wire, "you should be able to remove it without damaging the local power source."

I slam the wire cutters down. "Who says that I want to remove it?"

"It was just a guess," she says.

"And why should I believe anything you say?" I ask. After all, Astra thinks she's been lying to me for my own good, just like Mom and Dr. Ainge.

Her scowl could wither dandelions—if there were any left to wither. "I was *trying* to protect you. And I finally did come clean—at my own personal risk."

"You *think* you came clean," I reply, "but you're as hoodwinked as the rest."

"What is that supposed to mean?"

I duck my head. "Nothing." I hope I haven't said too much.

Astra plops down onto a barstool. "So what are we trying to do?"

I send her a sideways glance. Astra certainly isn't taking no for an answer, but then, neither am I. And it's not like I have to trust her with the details of my plan. As long as I keep mouth shut, I can take advantage of her skills.

"The last time I modified it, I maxed out the battery. Now I'm more interested in . . . speed."

Astra nods knowingly. "I've heard the low-grav races at the silo are insane."

"Low-grav races?" I reply.

She sends me a sideways glance. "If you're not entering the races, why are you tripping out your hoverboard?"

I see the trap she's set too late. Without answering her question, I snip the red-and-white-striped wire. Thankfully she doesn't try to squeeze any more information out of me, just hands me the right tools before I even know I need them. Once we've disentangled the capacitor and rerouted the power, she claps me on the back and melts back into the night.

# 26

ONCE THE HOVERBOARD IS FINISHED, I move on to my next task. I can't amass space bags at home without making Mom suspicious, so I plan to pack one at a time, then transport them to the roof of the observation tower for safekeeping. There's a decent chance Astra will stumble across them, but I plan to hide them well. And better her than Mom.

We're still doing a great job of avoiding one another, so I don't even feed Mom an excuse, just wrench the space bag from my closet and sneak it out to the garage. This one's got my solar blanket and a bunch of packets of space food. According to the labels, they can survive trips to both Venus *and* Uranus, so they should keep on the roof for a few days.

Main Street isn't far away, so I don't *need* the hoverboard, but I decide it wouldn't hurt to practice riding it with space bags. After drawing a deep breath, I wrap both arms around the space bag and step onto the hoverboard. It dips slightly beneath my weight, and I nearly tumble off.

A brittle haze dangles over Armstrong Street as I hover down the driveway and disappear into the night. Clouds scud across the sky like rows of kids playing leapfrog, and for a second, maybe more, I wish that I were one of them. That I had someone, lots of someones, I could turn to, rely on. But that's ridiculous, of course. I have no one. Less than no one.

By the time I reach the gate, I'm in no mood to play games. Branislav lurks in the guardhouse, menacing despite the nose hairs sticking out of both nostrils. I could have slithered through the gap in the Brandts' scraggly hedge, but I'm tired of hiding—from myself and from the world.

He glances at the time when I pull up to his window. "Getting kind of late for a joyride, isn't it?"

"Oh, this isn't a joyride. I'm getting ready for a mission."

Leering, Branislav props his elbows on the ledge. "And what mission would that be?"

"The *Juan Ponce de Léon's*," I say. "I'm tagging along to find my dad."

Branislav waits for me to laugh, then, when I just stand there staring, slaps his knee and cackles loudly. "Oh, that's rich, young man. *So* rich."

I force myself to grin. Of course he thinks it's just a joke. He, like everyone, assumes that Dad is dead and gone.

"I knew I liked you, Jameson." He presses the one button that the program trusts him with, and the heavy iron gate starts to swing out of the way. "Bring some space rocks back for me!"

I don't bother to respond, just smile smugly to myself and make the turn onto Main Street. Why lie when the truth is even less believable?

My arms are getting tired from holding on to the space bag, but I just have a little farther—fifty yards, then twenty-five, and then, suddenly, I'm there. As soon as the alley swallows me, I drop the space bag with a grunt. It kicks up a cloud of dust almost thick enough to chew.

I cough despite myself, then clap a hand over my mouth. But no one jumps out of the shadows to grill me on what I'm doing. In fact, the only thing that stirs is the Brandts' hedge across the street.

The hedge that hides the creaky gate that I *know* Astra's used before.

I hunker down behind my space bag, keeping my eyes fixed on the hedge. If Astra followed me, my tofu is as good as cooked. She'll take me down without a fight—or worse, race home to tell her dad.

A bead of sweat rolls down my nose. Then another. Then another. It doesn't take me long to speckle the outside of my space bag with dozens of sweaty dots. But Astra still hasn't shown, and the hedge hasn't stirred again. I must be getting paranoid.

Scrubbing the wetness off my nose, I pick the space bag up again, sling it across my back, and turn to face the ladder. I grab the highest rung that I can reach, then pull my legs up under me. I'm only halfway up when my arms start to feel like string beans. Instead of giving up, I concentrate on my end goal. Dad *needs* me to climb this wall. If I can't make it up this ladder, he'll be stuck on Mars forever.

Once I reach the top, it isn't hard to hide the space bag. The roof looks like a dumping ground for random hunks of junk. After stuffing my space bag under an old reflector panel, I dust off my gritty hands and climb back over the ledge. A sharp wind fans the trails of sweat carving furrows down my back, but it also makes me feel less stable. Suddenly I'm grateful for the thin layer of grit that's still clinging to my palms.

Even without the space bag, it's harder to climb down than it was to climb up. I can't see where I'm going or even where I've been, and when my foot slips off one rung, I lunge to catch myself, snagging my wrist on a loose screw.

Swallowing a cry for help, I grit my teeth and keep going. I can't store my stuff up here if I can't make it back down. Miraculously I make it to the bottom in one piece.

I climb back onto my hoverboard and sail away, away, away, flying down the middle of Main Street as fast as it will go. The wind blows sand and other bits of debris into my eyes, but that's not what's bugging me.

What's bugging me is that I can still feel someone's gaze pinging sharply off my back.

# 27

THREE DAYS LATER, I WAKE UP to the shushing of a gentle breeze. At first the sound is vaguely soothing, but then the details of last night come back—fell into bed, set the alarm, didn't fall asleep for hours—and I snap fully awake.

It's launch day, *the* launch day, and I slept through my alarm.

I throw the covers back and jerk the blinds out of the way. The light is still pale yellow, but the sun is fully up. A glance at my alarm clock confirms that it's 7:17. The launch is scheduled for 12:10, and I need at least five hours to gather my stuff, get to the launch site, and infiltrate the cargo hold. But as long as I don't run into any major snags, I think I can still salvage the mission.

I shuck off my pajamas and throw on the pants and shirt I laid out for myself the night before. They're made of alpaca wool and should keep me warm and toasty in the spaceship's cargo hold. I thought I'd need a space suit to survive the trip to Mars, but thankfully I remembered something— before he left for Mars, Dad trained with long-term sleeping pills. They're designed to put your body into a sub-comatose state, meaning it needs nowhere near as many resources to stay alive. After rooting around in the back of the medicine cabinet, I found his leftover stash.

I can't come up with a reason to do something with my hair, but I do take the extra time to both floss and brush my teeth. The *Juan Ponce de León* should only need three or four months to make it all the way to Mars, but that's still a long time to go without proper dental hygiene.

I'm spitting out my fluoride rinse when Mom shuffles past the bathroom. Ever since the truth came out—or what she thinks is the truth—she's morphed into a zombie. Her cheeks have grown more sunken, and she moves like someone switched her bones out for thick lead rods. She acts less like a mom and more like a scatterbrained roommate, but at least she's finally stopped trying to apologize.

The sight of my tooth-brushing must rouse some maternal instinct, because her forehead crinkles and she manages to ask, "Have you eaten breakfast yet?"

"Not yet," I reply. I'm planning to scarf down a breakfast bar on my way to the roof, but there's no way I'm adding that.

Mom half nods, half shrugs, as if I must know what I'm doing, and I think I'm off the hook. But then her glassy eyes narrow, and she peers more closely at my face.

"You look a little flushed," she says, pulling drawers open automatically. Can she really not remember where the thermometer is? "Are you coming down with something?"

"I'm fine," I say.

She half nods, half shrugs again. "Well, at least it's a launch day."

That makes me feel a little better. At least she knows it's a launch day. At least a part of her remembers that we don't have work or school, that I can stay home and recover.

Not that I plan to stay home.

Mom turns to go, then turns right back. "I love you, Jameson," she says, and for a second, maybe less, she almost sounds like Mom again.

Tears sting the backs of my eyes as I watch her stumble off. "I love you too," I croak, not loud enough for her to hear. For a brief moment, I'm tempted not to go. How can I leave her here alone? She can barely take care of herself.

I guess I'll just have to find Dad so he can take care of her instead.

Despite my awful start, I manage to make it to the alley only eight minutes behind schedule. There are gobs of people on Main Street drifting toward the school, so I'm going to have to be sneaky if I don't want to get caught. Luckily hanging out with Astra has taught me a few tricks.

Step one: Murder time while I wait for a break in the foot traffic. No one just hangs out on the sidewalk anymore—it's too dangerous to loiter underneath the toxic sun—so I have to come up with excuses to keep staying in one place. First I drop my tag. Then, while I'm picking it up, I notice my shoe is untied. But it's not really untied, so I have to untie and retie it, and since I'm already down here, I may as well untie and retie the other shoe too.

Step two: Slip into the alley at the first available moment. While I'm tying my shoes, I secretly survey the street. A smiling family on the opposite sidewalk has just passed my position, but a woman with her head down is right on top of me. It looks like she's focused on her commie, so as soon as she's past the alley, I make a break for the ladder. She doesn't even look up.

Step three: Get my butt up this ladder as fast as humanly possible. The alley is cloaked in shadow, so it's not nearly as warm as it was on the street. I press my forehead against the lowest rung, relishing its cool touch. My pulse never slows down, but it's probably going to get harder from here, so I force myself to climb.

I've been up and down this ladder multiple times in the past week, but scaling the dang thing hasn't gotten any easier. My palms still start to sweat within the first three or four rungs. They must be extra slippery today, because I've only secured my second handhold when one of them slips off. I manage to catch myself, but still. Maybe I should have picked a hiding place a little closer to the ground.

After wiping off my hand, I make a play for the next rung, but I've only just grabbed it when a harsh voice demands, "What are you doing up there?"

I sneak a peek under my arm. An angry-looking man is standing at the mouth of the alley, half in, half out of the sun. I knew that someone might test me, so I know what to do. Everyone takes a confident person seriously.

"Routine maintenance," I say, mimicking his deeper voice. Thanks to the vertical distance, he shouldn't be able to tell that I'm a kid.

"On a launch day?" the man asks.

I swallow, hard. He wasn't supposed to test me *twice*. "I'm afraid the air ducts don't know it's a launch day," I say, though my voice cracks on the last word. I clear my throat and try again: "So would it be all right if you just . . . left?"

"Not gonna happen," the man says, pulling out his souped-up commie. "I'm a block manager, you know, so I'm gonna need to see your tag and your proof of employment."

"Oh, it's gonna happen," a voice says from somewhere overhead, "because this is *my* block and *you're* interfering with an urgent work order."

The man and I crane our necks to catch a glimpse of the newcomer, though I don't need to see to know who the voice belongs to.

Astra.

# 28

MY HEART KICKS INTO OVERDRIVE, but Astra doesn't hesitate.

"I happen to be a district supervisor, so if you don't stand down, I'm gonna need to see *your* tag and your proof of employment."

The man's shoulders hunch. "My apologies," he mumbles, blinking against the sun's harsh glare. It looks like he's going to leave, but then he squints up at Astra. "Who did you say your program leader was?"

"I didn't!" she thunders as she points down the street.

The man scampers off without a backward glance, leaving me nowhere to go but up. Though I've scaled this wall a dozen times without her, Astra still hauls me up as soon as she can grab my collar. For a long time, we just stand there gasping, plainly gaping at each other.

"Thanks for your help back there," I mumble as I motion toward the alley, "but you should go home now—or at least to the launch party."

"Not gonna happen," Astra says, mimicking the man she just ran off. When I don't even crack a smile, she folds her arms across her waist. "Did you really think I wouldn't notice all the gear you stashed up here?"

I freeze despite myself. I knew it was a risk, but even *if* she found the space bags, I never thought she would confront me.

While I'm still fumbling for an answer, Astra stalks across the roof to the old reflector panel I've been stashing space bags under and chucks it aside. My top-secret stash glitters in the morning sun.

"I'm going . . . camping," I say lamely, scratching the back of my head. I've never been camping before, but I've heard it's something our ancestors used to do for fun.

Astra tugs a space bag open, revealing packets of space food.

"With lightweight rations," I add.

"Come on, Jameson," she says, cinching the space bag back up. "Don't play innocent with me. I figured out your plan last week."

"Who's playing innocent?" I ask. I've spent the past couple of weeks hiding everything from everyone, and now it all comes pouring out. "They've sent four other missions to that good-for-nothing planet, but they've never found the bodies. If you think my dad is dead, then you're as stupid as they are. And when I find him, you'll be sorry."

Astra doesn't reply, just calmly wipes my spit off her face.

"Did you hear what I said?" I ask, sticking my face right in her face. "I'm going to Mars to find my dad, and no one is going to stop me!"

Astra rolls her eyes. "I'm not here to stop you, moron. I'm here to go with you." She holds up a space bag of her own. "Did you really think I'd let you leave the planet without me?"

She couldn't have surprised me more if she'd punched me in the stomach. I look back and forth between Astra's face and the space bag, then, against my better judgment, throw my arms around her shoulders.

I draw a shaky breath as I stumble back a step. "Are we really going to do this?"

"I think we are," Astra replies.

The first thing we need to do is get our gear down to the ground. Now that the launch party has started, the sidewalks are mostly clear, so we shouldn't have a problem chucking space bags off the roof.

Sending Astra a small smirk, I retrieve her lonely space bag and throw it over the edge. At first she just stands there, stunned, but when her space bag hits the ground, she retaliates by dropping one of mine over the edge. At that point it becomes a full-on race, but when she dives for the space bag that contains the oxygen, I quickly jump in front of her.

"No, not that one!" I say sharply. I brought those sleeping pills, but if they aren't long-term enough, we're going to need that oxygen.

Astra understands at once. "I can take it then," she says, holding out her skinny arms. When I hesitate, she clucks her tongue. "I'm the better climber, and you know it."

I do know it, so I reluctantly hand over the space bag.

Against all odds, we reach the ground without breaking anything. While Astra slings space bags over and across her shoulders, I pry up the grate at the back of the alley. I waited until last night to hide the hoverboard, but I'm still relieved to see it here, waiting patiently for me. I took it out for a test run a couple of nights ago, and it clocked in at a sizzling 29 miles per hour. Since the launch site is only twelve miles away—four miles past Murphyville—we should make it there in no time.

Except I wasn't counting on hauling a second person.

I look Astra up and down. "How much do you weigh?"

She sticks both hands on her hips. "What kind of a question is *that*?"

"I need to recalculate our ETA"—I pull out my calculator—"but to do *that*, I need to know the weight of the expected load."

"Oh, just put that thing away." Astra disappears behind the oversized recycler at the back of the alley, returning with her turquoise bike. "I brought my own ride."

I know better than to protest. "Are you sure you can keep up?"

"Don't ever doubt the Turquoise Terror." She balances two space bags on the ends of her handlebars. "You might hurt its feelings."

"Your bike has a name? How did I not know this?"

Astra shrugs. "You never asked." And with that, she whips around, showering me with a fine spray of gravel.

I can't help but grin as I mount my hoverboard. Having Astra on this trip is going to make it ten times better.

# 29

NEXT STEP: GET OFF THE BASE. The Marines at the main gate are more for show than for security, but they still check everyone, and I seriously doubt they're going to let two fifth graders simply stroll through the main gate.

Fortunately there's a depot not far from Wheelock Park. It's where they stash the heavy vehicles, like moving vans and medi-tanks, when no one's using them. The depot isn't much to look at—a machine shop in the back, a foreman's hut out front, and a truck yard in the middle—

but it also isn't crowded. We should have no problem sneaking onto a supply truck without being spotted.

As soon as we get there, we spot a handy-dandy split in the depot's chain-link fence. After squirming through the split and crouching down well out of view of the trucks' apparent drivers, Astra spreads out the space bags and makes herself comfortable, but I'm too antsy to sit. I pace back and forth along the length of a supply truck.

Astra guzzles down another mouthful of water. "How will we know which truck to get on?"

"You know, you should really try to conserve our resources," I say, but it's more of an avoidance tactic than a genuine concern. "And if you want to know the truth, I figured there would be a sign."

"Please tell me you devoted at least some of that brainpower to sneaking onto our spaceship. I really don't want to get vaporized because you don't know the difference between a cargo hold and a freaking rocket booster."

My nostrils shrivel into slits. "I've had this spaceship sketched and modeled since before it was produced. Trust me when I say that boarding it *won't* be a problem."

She holds her hands up. "Great, I get it, you're a genius." She snaps her canteen closed and returns it to her space bag. "But that doesn't solve our current problem."

start laughing, Astra darts across the gap and hoists herself into the bed. I count to ten, then twenty, while I wait for her to stick her head back out and give me the all-clear.

I'm about to make a run for it when something—Astra's hand—motions sharply toward the tailgate. *Move, move, move!* it seems to say.

It doesn't have to tell me twice. With as much speed as I can muster, I wheel over Astra's bike, still toting two space bags, and lift it up to her. Astra's hands dart out to grab it, but not quickly enough—before she can secure it, the back wheel thunks against the tailgate.

I freeze instinctively, but no one comes around to investigate. After drawing a deep breath, I pass up my hoverboard.

I still have three space bags to transfer when the truck shudders and the pitch of the engine slides from low to high. The driver must have shifted. I glance up at the tailgate, then down at the last three space bags, frozen with indecision.

Astra sticks her head under the tarp. "Come *on*, Jameson," she hisses, holding out a sweaty hand. "What are you waiting for?"

Her familiar attitude unfreezes me. I grab two of the space bags, seize her outstretched hand, and leap. The massive tires start to roll just as she heaves me into the bed. Between my legs, her arms, and the supply truck's momentum, I can't help but go flying into a sack of corn. It isn't until I untangle myself that I realize I've lost another space bag.

Astra realizes it at the same time I do. Without saying a word, we press our eyes to the tarp's grommets, which serve as little portholes. Sure enough, our lost space bags are lying limply in the dirt like two desiccated slugs. The foreman approaches cautiously and, after nudging one of them, sends our supply truck a long look.

"What was in those?" Astra asks.

I take stock of our supplies. "Only the DreamTent and the backup water tablets." But assuming the sleeping pills work, we shouldn't need any more water than what we brought in our canteens. "We should be able to get by."

Astra checks her commie, then settles back against a sack of corn. "Then it's smooth sailing from here. As long as we don't take the scenic route, we should get to the launch site a little after eleven, which will give us more than enough time to sneak into the cargo hold."

I grin despite myself. "It sounds like someone did her homework."

Smiling, Astra shrugs. "I had some downtime," she replies.

I lean back against a space bag and stick my hands behind my head. It's the one with the oxygen, but I pretend it's a lounger and try to visualize our route. The first left is clearly getting us out of the depot, so the next right must be taking us onto the road leading to the main gate.

When we rumble to a stop, then, several anxious minutes later, *chug-chug-chug* to life again, I assume we've made it through. For the first time since we got back from the Third Rock Galleria, it feels like things might be OK. I made a plan. I'm sticking to it. I even have a travel buddy.

Then I realize we're slowing down.

"What are they doing?" Astra whispers, cocking her head to the side.

"I don't know," I admit. If there's something in the road, they might get out to inspect it, so the last thing I want to do is out us as stowaways. "Taking a bathroom break, maybe?"

"Doubtful," she replies as she creeps over to the tailgate. I don't know what she plans to do if they fling that tarp out of the way, but she's clearly gearing up for something.

My tongue feels as thick as an old sock, but my mouth's too dry to swallow. It can't end here. It *won't*. I tense, prepared to spring, but before we stop completely, everything tilts to the side. Yelping, Astra tumbles into another sack of corn, but when the world shifts by a right angle, I realize what's going on.

"We're turning."

# 30

I LEARNED LOTS OF THINGS on our trip to the galleria, one of which is that the dusty road to Murphyville is as straight as a vector. We shouldn't be swerving, let alone making a right turn. It's too late for stealth now, so I stick my head under the tarp and spot the main gate not behind us but directly over to our right.

"This is bad," I say as I slide my head back in. I kick the tailgate for good measure. "Where do these supply trucks think they're going?"

"Not to the launch site," Astra says. "Which means we're gonna have to bail."

"What do you mean, 'bail'?" I ask.

She hands me a space bag, then sets my hoverboard on top of it. "Let me see if I can put it in the simplest possible terms—we're gonna jump out of this truck and hope like heck we can still walk."

I roll my tongue around my mouth. "I don't think I can do that."

"Well, you're gonna *have* to do it if you want to make that launch." Astra slings a pair of space bags over her shoulders. "And you're gonna have to do it before this truck picks up more speed."

I cling to the space bag like a lifeline, then notice the Turquoise Terror. "You're leaving your bike behind?"

Sniffing, Astra nods. "It's not like we'll need it on Mars." Then she looks me in the eyes. "We're gonna go on three, OK? One, two, THREE!"

Not thinking, barely breathing, I throw myself over the tailgate. The world is suddenly too big, too bright, and I shut my eyes instinctively. Luckily the ground is a hard target to miss.

By the time I finish rolling, I honestly can't tell which way is up and which is down. When I crack one eye open, the only thing I can see is sand, which means I've rolled onto my stomach. I take a mental inventory of my aches and pains, then push myself onto my knees.

"You're bleeding," Astra says.

I check my hands, my feet, my elbows, but everything seems fine. Then I roll my tongue around my mouth and realize it tastes like old screws smell. "I must have bit my lip."

"Yeah, it looks pretty chewed up—no pun intended," she replies. A small smile splits her face, but it goes as quickly as it came. "You want me to patch you up? I'm pretty sure I brought a first-aid kit."

I knew I'd forgotten something. "That's all right. Let's just keep going." After making sure the trucks aren't stopping or slowing down, I dust off my hoverboard and nobly offer it to her. "Do you want to borrow it?"

She shakes your head. "You brought it this far. You should take it all the way."

After scooping up the three measly space bags we have left, we set off toward the launch site. The first thing that strikes me is how dead everything looks. I didn't notice on our drive to Murphyville, but now I realize how barren the landscape is. The sand dunes are lifeless, and even the clumps of sage look like they're barely holding on.

I've never been to the Great Waste, but it can't look much
worse than this.

The second thing that strikes me is how truly hot the
sun is, even with my solar jack and the ever-present wind.
Base Ripley may have dead grass, but it also has buildings
that partially obstruct the sun. Except for the thin black
stripes that hover under the sand dunes, shade is a distant
memory out here. I find I'm chugging water faster than I
thought I would.

And I'm not even walking.

"How . . . much . . . farther?" Astra asks as we pass yet
another clump of sage.

I toe the hoverboard's display. The gauge can toggle
back and forth between a speedometer and an odometer,
but the news isn't that good.

"Another three miles," I say with as much cheerfulness
as I can muster. I decide not to mention that that's only to
Murphyville.

Astra's shoulders sag. "Then I think I need to take
a break."

I don't have a chance to look around, let alone identify
a stopping point, before two space bags hit the ground.
I step back on the hoverboard, but I must step back too
hard, because it jerks to a stop. I half jump, half fall off,

but at least I don't fall down. By the time I turn around, Astra's laid out on the shoulder, breathing rapidly.

An alarm bell goes off in my head. "Do you need more water?" I ask.

"Yeah," Astra replies, reaching blindly for my canteen.

The hair on the back of my neck prickles. She can't be out of water. We still have miles to go. But instead of pumping her for information she's in no condition to give, I press my canteen to her lips. Her neck muscles convulse as the water pours down her throat.

"Thanks," she says tiredly once the water's mostly gone. "If you just give me a few minutes, I swear I'll be ready to go."

Without waiting for my answer, she drapes an arm over her face and promptly falls asleep. The sleeve of her solar jack reflects the morning sun, so I can't look at her for long, but that leaves me with nothing to do but count clumps of sage—and worry.

Everyone learns about sun poisoning from a very early age. Since we're closer to the sun, you now get irradiated from the excess UV rays, but you also get the rash and the dangerously high fever people used to get from heatstroke. There's nothing you can do to avoid the

UV rays but put on your solar jack, but you can avoid the symptoms that resemble good old heatstroke by taking it easy on yourself.

As opposed to walking through a desert for the past 45 minutes.

Astra's still out cold, but it's been more than six minutes, which was already six minutes more than we could afford to spare.

"Time to wake up, Astra." I nudge her with my toe. "We need to keep moving."

She doesn't even budge.

I shake her shoulder. "I said, it's time to wake up."

This time she groans and rolls over. "Five more minutes, Dad."

I tell myself she's just joking. "No more minutes," I reply as I force her to sit up. Deep down I'm terrified that she's going to slump over as soon as I let go, so I keep hold of her as she struggles to her feet.

"Oh right, the launch," she says, scrubbing her splotchy face.

"I'll take the space bags," I tell her. It's a command, not a suggestion. "And you'll ride the hoverboard."

I expect Astra to argue, but she just shoves the space bags off. "Be my guest," she says blithely as she mounts the hoverboard. It tilts dangerously at first, then slowly stabilizes as she finds what's left of her balance.

I tell myself not to freak out as I retrieve Astra's space bags. I already have one on my back, so I stick one on my front and tuck the third under my arm. But something's poking me, so I'm forced to rotate them, back to arm, arm to front, then, finally, front to back.

My rearranging's given Astra a good four-minute head start, but I catch up easily. According to the hoverboard, she's not even moving two miles per hour.

"More water?" Astra asks.

"Yeah, sure," I reply, even though I'm almost out.

She takes my canteen and tips her head back. Her lips are so swollen she can barely control them. "Thanks," is all she says as she hands it back to me.

I nod ruefully. This isn't how I thought this trip was going to unfold. Astra can barely stand up straight, and we're not even halfway there.

When the first house appears, I almost do a happy dance. Whoever lives in that house must have access to water, and there's a big clothesline tree on the edge of the yard. It will be a great spot to rest.

I've gotten a few yards ahead, so I turn my head and ask, "Are you thinking what I'm thinking?"

When she doesn't answer, I sneak a peek over my shoulder. I don't know how I missed it, but Astra has collapsed.

# 31

I THROW OFF THE SPACE BAGS and get down on my hands and knees. For one heart-stopping moment, I'm sure that Astra's dead, but when I roll her over, I discover that she's breathing. In fact, she's almost panting.

"We're going to be all right," I say, more for my benefit than hers. "I'm going to take care of you."

But taking care of Astra is way easier said than done. I squint up and down the road, but there's no one else in sight. *I'm* the only help she's going to get at the moment.

A dozen lessons on sun poisoning file through my brain. The first thing I need to do is get Astra out of the sun. We may as well be ants under a magnifying glass out here. The house I spotted earlier is one sand dune away, a quarter of a mile at the most. I can drag her that far.

Can't I?

First I try the hoverboard, though I'm sure that it won't work. It's designed to carry a centered, upright load, so when Astra's arms and legs flop uselessly over the sides, the hoverboard sputters and dies. Next I grab her by the armpits and literally drag her across the sand. It works for ten or fifteen yards, but then my back gives out, quickly followed by my arms. I need more thrust, more leverage. If only I had a stretcher—or a spare solar jack.

As soon as that thought pops into my head, I strip off my solar jack and slide it under Astra's torso. The length of the sleeves gives me just enough leverage to get her moving again, so the next ten or fifteen yards are significantly easier than the last ten or fifteen were.

"Almost—there," I say between noisy gasps for breath, but it's an out-and-out lie. Several dozen yards may as well be several dozen miles when you're dragging someone through loose sand.

I force myself to focus on each step, not the overall distance, so when my back finally bumps into the weathered picket fence, I almost give it a big kiss. But then I remember I can't afford to waste my spit.

The sun beats down on my neck as I kick down a sagging fence post and drag Astra through the opening. Luckily the clothesline tree I spotted is in this corner of the yard. When I slide my solar jack out from under Astra's torso and drape it across the nylon cords, it creates a patch of shade.

I sink down into the dirt. "See, that wasn't so hard, was it?"

Astra's eyelids twitch. "Jameson?" she rasps.

"I'm right here, Astra," I reply as I grab hold of her hand. Her skin is hot and dry.

She tries to say something, but her mouth won't form the words. I pull out my canteen and let the last few drops fall into her eager mouth. Her tongue darts across her lips, lapping up every last dribble, before she coughs and murmurs, "More?"

She took the words right out of my mouth. I survey the surrounding yard through narrowed eyes, then retrieve my canteen.

"I'll be right back," I say determinedly.

The ever-present wind feels pleasant on my clammy skin as I dash up the walkway and pound on the front door. I knock *and* ring the doorbell, but no one comes to answer it. Whoever lives in this old place must be partying in Murphyville. Apparently launch days aren't just holidays for us.

I think about throwing a rock through one of the curtained windows and leaving a quick note—"I don't have any paper money, but if you want a new window, please ask the commissary to charge it to Jameson O'Malley's account"—but then I think better of it. I've become a little squeamish about breaking and entering. I will if I have to, but there must be another way.

After ringing the doorbell one last time, I climb over the railing and circle the house. It looks like this place used to be an outdoor shadehouse, because there's a field out back dominated by a rusty tractor. I poke my head into the barn, but the only things inside it are a collection of odd tools and an old, gas-powered motorcycle with an almost empty tank. Shaking my head, I close the door. The motorcycle might have helped if Astra had been able to ride it.

Dry weeds and rotting seedpods crunch beneath my feet as I circle the barn. I need to go back and check on Astra, but I don't want to go back empty-handed. Unfortunately there's nothing back here but another picket fence, another rusty tractor, and an outhouse.

An outhouse?

Murphyville may be backward, but it's not like we live in the Middle Ages. I creep closer to the outhouse, sniffing the air experimentally. There's the normal smell of dust and a hint of something more, but I guess that makes sense. Certainly outhouses are supposed to smell like *something*.

When I reach the door, I hesitate. Someone has cleared the rotting seedpods that dot the rest of the yard, and the bushy weeds poking up between the boards are actually alive. Plus the shiny lock looks new. Who installs a new old-fashioned lock on an outhouse they shouldn't have to use?

The answer to that question is easy—someone who has something to hide.

I push the door halfheartedly, but of course, it's locked. Next I test the strength of the flimsy-looking wall, but the warped wooden boards are surprisingly sturdy.

Anxiety stirs in my stomach as I consider getting past them, but then I think of Astra and her determination to come with me. Whatever this house's secrets are, I have to unlock them for her sake.

My skin no longer feels clammy as I tromp back to the barn—if anything, it's started to itch—but I force myself to ignore it as I throw open the doors. The barn's darkened interior momentarily blinds me, but after my pupils adjust, the first thing that comes into focus is a long-handled ax.

Bingo.

The ax sounds like a lightning bolt biting into the outhouse, but no one comes out to scold me. It only takes me a few swings to create a head-sized hole in the back wall. I brace myself for the reveal as I slide my head into the hole, but it's even better than I thought.

Someone built this outhouse around a water pump.

Thirst turns me into a wild animal as I widen the hole until it's big enough to fit through. A jagged corner nicks my arm as I struggle to get in, but I barely feel the pain as I prime the water pump and position my canteen for a refill.

When the water starts to flow, I only catch it in the canteen for a second, then let the canteen go and use my cupped hands instead. The water feels like silk and tastes like heaven, but as it splatters my shoes and turns the cracked, broken ground into a muddy mess, I realize how much I'm wasting—and how much Astra needs a drink.

Ignoring my own thirst, I pick up the canteen and hold it under the spigot until it's completely full, then screw the cap back on and clamber out of the outhouse. Precious drops land in the dirt as I race across the yard, leaving an incriminating trail from the outhouse to the clothesline tree, but the sun will lick them up before anyone can see them.

Astra is little more than a clump of dusty clothes by the time I get back to her, and I suck a sharp breath through my teeth. Luckily her eyelids flutter before I'm forced to check her vitals.

"You came back," she says.

"Of course I did," I say as I unscrew the canteen's cap. My fingers feel stiff, so it takes me a few tries. "And I brought you a surprise."

Her eyes don't even brighten at the sight of the canteen, but at least she drinks, though every swallow makes her grimace. I only get her to drink half before she turns her head away. I sit back on my heels and wait for her to magically get better, but as the seconds tick away, Astra doesn't get any better. If anything, she gets worse.

"Thank you," Astra slurs as her eyes slide shut again. "I think I . . . needed . . . that."

"Don't go to sleep," I say as I jiggle her shoulder. I may not have a proper ice bath, but I can at least keep her awake.

When her eyes don't open, I force myself to pinch her. "I said, don't go to sleep."

She manages to frown. "How can I . . . go to sleep . . . with you pinching . . . my shoulder?"

I can't help but laugh. "Keep the attitude coming. And while you're taking potshots at me, why don't you take another drink?"

Astra grimaces, but when I hold up the canteen, she does take another sip. "Instead of accosting me with your canteen, why don't you tell me what you found?"

Eager to keep her talking, I tell her about my misadventures, working backward from the water pump to the outhouse to the barn. When I get to the motorcycle, she actually struggles to sit up.

"Whoa there," I say, pressing her shoulders back down. I don't have to press too hard. "Where do you think you're going?"

"Motorcycle," Astra croaks. "If I can get it running, you can still make it to the launch."

I turn my thumb toward my chest. "Still can't ride a bike, remember? And even if I could, how could I abandon you? You can't even sit up straight."

Astra nails me with a glare. "I'm hardly helpless," she replies.

I shake my head sadly. She's three nuts short of a toolbox. "You're suffering from stage-three sun poisoning. To be honest, I don't know how we're even having this conversation."

Astra ignores me. "To get the motorcycle going, stick the key in the ignition, flip the engine shutoff switch to on, and press the power button."

"How do you know this stuff?" I ask.

"Small Engine Mechanics was a class at my old school." Astra draws a labored breath. "Make sure the engine is in neutral, or the dang thing might fall over. Once you get the engine running, shift the bike into first gear—grab the clutch with your left hand, work the gears with your right foot—and give it a little gas."

I bat that away. "For the last time, *I'm not going*." I absently unscrew the cap and tip the canteen toward her lips.

She presses them into a line. "Well, if you *won't* go, then I won't take another sip." The water splashes off her chin.

"That's blackmail," I reply.

"Take it or . . . leave it," she says. It comes out as a breathy whistle, and her head lolls to the side. "You'll never get a better chance."

The anger rushes out of me in one big whoosh. She came on this doomed trip for *me*. Now she's abandoning it for me too.

Reluctantly I slide the canteen between her blistering hands, then push myself back to my feet and stagger over to the barn. The doors are still wide open, so all I have to do is disengage the kickstand and climb onto the seat. I'm a lot taller than I was the last time I tried to ride a bike, so my feet still touch the ground.

As I go through Astra's checklist, a part of me hopes it won't turn on. But as soon as I press the power button, the engine roars to life. The motorcycle snarls threateningly as I grip the clutch and slowly ease into first gear, then rockets out of the barn as soon as the flywheel catches. Somehow I squeeze the brake, shift down into neutral, and get my feet back on the ground before the stupid thing tips over.

Once I can hear the engine growling over the gushing of my pulse, I blink my scratchy eyes and shift into first gear again. Since I'm expecting it this time, I manage to control the jolt, but I only let myself leap forward a couple of yards before I clamp down on the brake.

I need to choose, to act, but my heart and mind are frozen. With a case of stage-three sun poisoning, Astra won't live out the hour. But with no one looking for him, Dad will be missing forever. The motorcycle growls beneath me as my head whips back and forth. I can go on to the launch site or back to Base Ripley for help.

The launch site or Base Ripley.

Base Ripley or the launch site.

How can I choose between two of the people I love most?

I think back on the things Dad sacrificed to support *me*. Sleep when I was sick. Extra food when I was hungry. Free time to build the JICC and teach me how to play gravball.

Then, without warning, a memory rises to the surface. We were building the reflector dish when a tiny brown *something* rounded the corner of the house and skittered across our lava rocks. I yelped and rushed for Dad, who was more curious than scared. While I clambered onto a step stool, Dad crunched across the lava rocks and swept aside our oleander. A baby bird chirped mournfully.

Dad smiled and waved me over. He said it was called a quail and pointed out its injured wing. While he hunted for its mom, I studied the baby bird. It looked like a cotton ball that had been dipped in mud and dust, but it looked kind of cuddly too. When it cocked its tiny head to get a better look at me, my fear and doubt melted away.

We never found the mama bird—Dad guessed that she'd died from exposure—so we became its family. We ended up naming it Sage because we had no idea if it was a boy or a girl. Dad designed a tiny splint, I looked for bugs and stuff to feed it, and Mom mashed them into a paste. By the end of the month, Sage had quadrupled in size. It only took another month for its wing to finish healing.

As an eight-year-old, I thought that Sage would live with us forever. When Dad started to teach it how to run and hunt and fly so it could move back to the wild, my small heart split in half. Still, when Dad invited me to drive out to the dunes with him and return Sage to the desert, I knew that I couldn't say no.

We placed Sage in a shoebox, piled into the Light-Year, and rumbled out to Gurley's Dune. Dad found a secluded canyon thick with creosote bushes and a dried-up riverbed that probably flooded when it rained. He said it was the perfect spot.

I didn't agree. Who said we had to turn Sage loose? Sage was a part of our family. Why couldn't it just live with us?

*Because*, Dad said patiently, *we love it too much to keep it. Sage was never meant to live in a shoebox in a house. Sometimes loving something means that you have to let it go.*

I don't notice my eyes are closed until I open them again and remember where I am. Not standing at the mouth of Sage's secluded canyon but staring up and down a road that can only take me back or forward. Salty tracks make my cheeks itch, though the tears that produced them have long since evaporated.

I know what I have to do.

With the decision finally made, I feel as light as a balloon. When I let go of the brake, the motorcycle leaps ahead, and this time, I let it go. I'm down the dusty driveway and back onto the road before I realize I'm moving. The clothesline tree is dead ahead, and then it's there, and then it's past. Just thinking about turning my head makes the motorcycle wobble, so I don't try to look for Astra. She doesn't need my eyes now, anyway; she needs my bravery.

The sandy landscape rockets past in a smear of grays and tans, so at first, I don't notice that my depth perception's off, that my vision is deteriorating. When my hand slips off the handlebar, the motorcycle wavers. Somehow I recover, but the beast's still slowing down. Whether the gas is running out or I can't put as much pressure on the pedals is irrelevant. I'm not going to make it.

Something shimmers in the distance. It could be a mirage, but even if it's not, the tiny corner of my brain that can still do calculations knows I'm not going to get there at this rate of speed.

When the motorcycle starts to wobble, a voice yells, *Get out of the way!* But even after I've gotten off and the motorcycle has toppled over, I just stand there staring. There must be something I can do to get it moving again, but for the life of me, I can't remember what it is.

Something thrashes uncontrollably at the back of my brain, but ignoring the something is easier than listening to it. Besides, I'm *so* tired, more tired than I've ever been. Or at least more tired than I've been in the past five minutes, and right now, those are the only ones I can remember.

Thankfully a patch of grass materializes at my feet as I lie down in the motorcycle's shade. The grass feels hot and gritty, more like sand than grass, but it's grass. It has to be. I've never seen anything this green.

The only bad thing about lying on this grass is the unrelenting sun. I raise a hand to shield my eyes, which draws my attention to my arm. Why is my arm red? It's supposed to be another color. I can't remember which color at the moment, but I know it isn't red.

It's only once the darkness starts to embrace me from behind, sweeping across my field of vision like the ocean I've never seen, that I remember why my arm is as red as Mars' dirt. It's because my solar jack is currently in a clothesline tree, spreading shadows over Astra.

I hope it takes better care of her than it did of me.

# 32

I WAKE UP IN A COCOON. It doesn't feel as velvety as grass, but it's a heck of a lot softer than sand. I'm not sure if I'm alive, but when I try to raise my arm and my muscles won't respond, I decide that I must be. If death is this restrictive, then I want my money back.

I crack one eye open, and light hits my retina for the first time in a long time. As I blink instinctively, the world comes back into focus. The tiny spaceships don't make any sense at first, but when I spot the JICC, I know exactly where I am.

"Jamie?" someone peeps. My head's still turning toward the sound—sluggishly, effortfully—when two familiar arms wrap themselves around my neck. "Oh, Jameson."

Mom's arms feel like sandpaper on my tender skin, and I can't help but wince. She jerks back automatically, taking several layers of skin with her.

"Oh, Jamie, I'm so sorry." But then her words catch up to her, and she presses her lips into a line. More quietly she asks, "Can I do anything for you?"

"Water?" I manage to croak.

Mom lunges for the nightstand, but my head's too thick to turn. Then a straw lands in my mouth, and while I suck and suck and suck, she holds the glass and asks, "Better?"

I nod gratefully. But even nodding hurts.

She sets the glass back on the nightstand and pretends to fix my sheets. "Do you need anything else?"

*A tofu taco would be nice, and a skin transplant, if you're offering,* are the words I want to say. But the thought of forcing them through my dried-up vocal chords is enough to make me sweat, so I wince and shake my head.

She tries to take hold of my hand, then notices the chapped red skin and returns hers to her lap instead. "Oh, Jameson," she peeps. "Can you ever forgive me?"

I think back on all the things she probably feels guilty for. For not telling me about the crash, then for telling me the way she did, then for becoming a zombie. Then I think back on all the things I'm not especially proud of either, and the list seems ten times longer, ten times more difficult to work through.

"How can I not?" I ask.

A single tear slides down Mom's cheek, and I have to close my eyes to keep my own from surfacing. I don't need to add itch to injury right now.

She pats the tips of my hair. "When did you become the grown-up?"

I try to stay awake, to keep our conversation going. I know I'm forgetting something—something big, something important—but I can't remember what. And I *am* monstrously tired.

I'm on the verge of drifting off when Astra's face swims into view. Astra was the one with me. *Astra* was the one in trouble. I blurt her name instinctively as I sit straight up in bed.

Mom presses her lips into a line, but I refuse to accept it. Astra *has* to be OK. I'm about to throw my covers back and somehow roll out of my bed when Mom leans back just far enough to let me catch a glimpse of the doorway—and the familiar girl leaning casually against the doorframe.

Astra's clothes are clean and barely wrinkled, and for once her hair is down. Her hands and arms are swathed in bandages, but when I meet her eyes, she smiles a full-mouthed, gap-toothed smile that I've never seen before.

"I'll get some cookies," Mom whispers, pushing herself back to her feet. Her footsteps are as quiet as a sigh as she slips around Astra and disappears into the hall.

Even after Mom is gone, Astra doesn't say a word, just pads across the worn carpet and lowers herself into my desk chair. Then we just stare at one another. I can't believe she's here. I can't believe she's *fine*. I guess my solar jack really did take better care of her.

But Astra's not content to stare. She opens and closes her mouth—starting, stopping, starting, stopping—and I get the impression that she wants to say something nice but can't quite bring herself to do it. So when her hands clench into fists and she punches me in the shoulder, hard, I can honestly say that I didn't see it coming.

I don't know how to react. My shoulder may be one of my least injured body parts, but still. You don't just punch the person who risked his life to save yours; it's kind of an unwritten rule. I'm about to say so too when I spy the single tear gathering in the corner of her eye. I manage to choke back the words that have been forming in my throat.

"What were you *thinking?*" she demands.

I don't know how to answer that. "You're going to have to be more specific. What was I thinking *when?*"

"You could have made it," she goes on, thoroughly ignoring me. "Dad told me afterward that a minor system crash caused a *two-hour* delay. You could have gotten to the launch." She gulps. "So why did you go *back?*"

I think about it for a while, then, finally, tell her the truth: "Because I realized that going back was going forward in my case." When she just blinks, I shrug. "Besides, you weren't looking great, and it's not like you have a bubbly personality to fall back on."

Astra half laughs, half sobs, then carefully dries off her face and not-so-carefully punches me in the other shoulder. "You know, I might just keep these bandages. They make great boxing gloves." Her grin is quick and sharp, but it fades as quickly as it came. "How can I ever repay you?"

I feel the heat crawl up my neck. "How can *I* ever repay *you?*"

Because she didn't just come with me, didn't just believe in me. She *understood* what it was like to want a missing parent back. What kinds of risks you'd take. Deep down she must have known that I was chasing an illusion, but she let me keep believing right until the very end.

I'm so glad *we* didn't end.

The corners of Astra's mouth curl up as she returns the desk chair to the JICC. "Oh, I'm sure we'll think of something." After jiggling the mouse and fiddling with the keyboard, she tiptoes out into the hall.

It's only once she's gone that I realize she typed in *DOWNLOAD*.

"She fixed the JICC," I breathe. Then I say it again, louder: "Astra, you fixed the JICC!"

She doesn't have a chance to answer before I notice that the pixels are rearranging themselves into an image.

An image of Dad.

"Is this thing on?" he asks, fumbling with something I can't see. "OK, I guess it's on." He draws a bracing breath, then looks directly at the camera. "How are you doing, kid?"

Dad looks the same but different. Longer, maybe. Slightly thinner. The walls surrounding him are vaguely rounded instead of square and flat. I don't recognize the backdrop, a complicated mix of knobs and buttons. In the top right corner of the image is an oblong porthole, and in the top right corner of that porthole is a brightly glowing star.

He doesn't have to tell me it's the sun.

"You must know by now that the JICC never really worked." This longer, thinner Dad clings to a built-in bar for balance. "It can send messages OK, but it doesn't know how to receive them. I knew that we were almost there, that we had one last hoop to jump through, but I was out of time." He drags a hand under his nose. "I'm sorry for misleading you—and for asking your mom to go along with my harebrained scheme. Please don't be mad at her. I just wanted you to have something from *me*."

Dad lowers his gaze, and I can't help but blink back tears. It takes me a few seconds to realize that's what he's doing too.

"But if you're watching this," he says as his stormy eyes brighten, "you must have found a way to fix it. I always knew you would, which is why I'm sending this transmission." His smile is proud. "You always were a special kid."

At this I picture Astra toiling away with blistered hands. I picture Mom trying to help and Mr. Primm trying to keep Janus from destroying everything, and for some reason, I laugh. They did all this for me. They couldn't have known about the message, but they did it anyway.

If I'm a special kid, it's only because I have a special family.

Dad's gaze drifts around the cabin. "As for me, I'm hanging in. It's day one-oh-eight up here, so we're all getting kind of restless. Lincoln has started playing chess with one of the IT guys back home—it takes them days to finish a game with the delay—and Winter doesn't just listen to Puccini anymore, she gives us a full concert every night."

Their faces march across my brain as he rattles off their names. I remember meeting Winter a few days before the launch. She gave me her lucky snakeskin for safekeeping. I wish I could remember where I put it.

"The good news is that Haisheng says we're well ahead of schedule, so we should be able to begin our Martian rendezvous procedures within the next couple of days." Dad tucks his hands behind his head and lets himself bob up and down. "Rendezvous isn't my rodeo, but once we touch down, the baton will pass to me. Once we entrench the pods and establish a perimeter, the next item of business will be to set up the equipment so we can start transmitting data. That should take four to eight weeks, so I probably won't be able to upload any more videos for the next month or two." He grabs hold of the built-in bar and reels himself back in. "So if you don't hear from me, don't go and blab to Mom. I don't want you guys freaking out."

A single tear slides down my cheek.

"Take care of yourself," Dad says as his longer-than-normal curls float around his head like a halo. "And take care of your mom. She needs you more than you know." He looks up at the porthole, then back down at the controls. Anywhere but at the camera. "I love you, kid. I always will. See you on the other side." He reaches for the kill switch, then remembers to add at the last second, "*Amerigo Vespucci* to Jameson."

The monitor expands to white, and then the cursor pops back up. It blinks expectantly, a centimeter-long beacon of hope, but I no longer need a centimeter's worth of hope. I have a whole galaxy's.

"I love you too. Earth to Dad."

# Acknowledgments

First, thank you to Brent Taylor, who saw something worth pursuing in two very different stories. Your enthusiasm is infectious, and your tireless work ethic is a wonder to behold. I wouldn't be where I am today without your great representation.

Second, thank you to Alison Deering, whose interest in my writing renewed my faith in myself. I was beginning to wonder if I'd ever sell another manuscript, but you put those fears to rest. I don't doubt this story landed precisely where it was meant to. Many thanks also to the entire Capstone team, especially Beth Brezenoff, Nick Healy, and Tracy McCabe, who knocked it out of the park when she brought Jen Bricking in to illustrate. The cover turned out beautifully.

Every writer needs a slew of insightful writer friends who can pinpoint lots of problems and come up with ways to fix them. For this book, those writer friends were Ben Spendlove, Jenilyn Collings, and Myrna Foster (with some extra thanks to Ben, whose stories inspire *me* and who dreamed up a climax that was way better than mine). I'm also grateful for writer friends who respond to whiny emails and keep me from going crazy, including but not limited to Elizabeth Briggs, Liesl Shurtliff, and Mónica Bustamante Wagner.

Thank you to my parents, Gary and Linda Van Dolzer, who gave me not just a name but the confidence to pursue my dreams. Thanks also to Kate Testerman for her feedback on the first few chapters and to Dr. Samuel Tolley for his help building the JICC. I probably still messed some things up, but if I got anything right, it was surely thanks to you.

Finally, thank you to Chris, who doubles every joy and halves every disappointment, and to Isaac, Madeleine, and William, who love me even when I have to do "computer things." I wouldn't want to make this journey with anyone but you. And to the unnamed gummy bear who I hope will have a name by the time this book comes out, thank you for simply existing.

# About the Author

Krista Van Dolzer is a stay-at-home mom by day and a children's author by bedtime. She lives with her husband and four kids in Layton, Utah, and hopes she doesn't have to move—to Mars or anywhere else—for at least several decades. Krista is also the author of *The Sound of Life and Everything* and *Don't Vote for Me*.